The Other Karen

Also by Velda Johnston

The Other Karen

Velda Johnston

DODD, MEAD & COMPANY, NEW YORK

Published by Dodd, Mead & Company, Inc.
79 Madison Avenue, New York, N.Y. 10016
Distributed in Canada by
McClelland and Stewart Limited, Toronto
Manufactured in the United States of America

FIRST EDITION

Library of Congress Cataloging in Publication Data

Johnston, Velda
    The Other Karen.

    I. Title
PS3560.039408   1983   813'.54   83-11562
ISBN 0-396-08248-3

For my sister-in-law, EMILIE C. MATHEWS

The Other Karen

CHAPTER 1

IF NEW YORK CITY that early summer had not begun to seem to me like a foretaste of hell, none of it would have happened. I would never have answered that ad in the *Village Voice*. And therefore later on I would not have stood on the shore of a wind-roughened Maine lake while a man I had never seen before tongue-lashed me for things I had never done. And still later, I would not have found myself in that desolate place three thousand miles away, with a desert wind rattling the stiff branches of a mesquite clump outside a baling wire fence, and distant mountains whose name I did not know rising black against a late afternoon sky.

I had not always felt depressed by New York City. When I had first come to it a half-dozen years earlier, a twenty-one-year-old fresh out of a small Kansas college, I'd loved it. As I suppose it does to any ambitious new-comer, the city seemed to me one gigantic crackerjack box filled with all sorts of prizes. The immediate

1

prize I hoped for was theatrical success. After all, hadn't my drama teacher said that my interpretation of Blanche DuBois in the college production of *Streetcar* was almost as good as Jessica Tandy's, whose Broadway performance she had seen years and years before?

Later on, I was sure, less glittering but equally important prizes would come my way. Marriage to some attractive and—in the phrase then current—upwardly mobile young man. Eventually a house in Connecticut or Long Island. A child, or perhaps even two, with some competent person to help raise them while I continued to reap praise from the drama critics.

That first magic year in New York everything delighted me, even the graffiti-covered subway cars. As they thundered into the gray underground stations, the blue stars and red suns and purple comets on their steel sides reminded me of a small circus that had visited Prairie Center, Kansas, when I was a child. The circus wagons had borne equally brilliant colors. As for big-city crime, the very knowledge that it would be unsafe for me to venture off well-lighted avenues into side streets after dark lent a certain added spice to life.

Temperatures sizzled that first summer I spent in New York, but I, ensconced in a tiny room at the Y, was unaware of discomfort. That winter, after I moved into a West Side apartment already occupied by two other aspiring actresses, the weather turned bitterly cold, but I didn't mind that either. Why should I, when everything else was going so well for me? I had work as an office temporary almost whenever I wanted it. And I'd been given a number of walk-on roles in soap operas. True, those parts were nonspeaking. True, those millions of TV viewers caught only a glimpse of me as, in a nurse's uniform, I got out of an elevator one of the leading characters was about to enter, or, in street clothes, climbed into a taxi one of the stars had just left. But sooner or later some director was going to say, "That girl playing one of the reporters in that last scene. What's her name? Catherine Mayhew? I think she's got something."

It would be only a matter of time.

But I had not dreamed that so much time could pass and still leave me waiting for that lightning flash—some TV director's taking notice of me, some theater audition resulting in a choice role—that would transform my life. Oh, a few things did happen. I moved out of the apartment I shared with those two other would-be actresses into my own furnished apartment on West Fourteenth Street. It was a cramped studio walkup, but at least its bathroom was not festooned perennially with pantyhose. Once in a while I'd spoken a line or two in some soap opera. ("The doctor will see you now, Mrs. Quartermaine," or, "No, officer, I didn't hear any disturbance in the apartment upstairs.") For several nights I actually did appear on stage in an off-off-Broadway revival of a nineteen-twenties farce. Most of the critics mercifully ignored it. But New York's most acidulous commentator upon the theater, drawn to the play as a mugger might be to a cripple, wrote: "A misguided group calling themselves the Footlighters have revived something called *Shipmates*. A decent respect for the dead should have made them leave undisturbed a play which was moribund even when it left its author's typewriter more than a half-century ago." *Shipmates* closed the night after his review appeared.

Most of the time my career proceeded as it had that first year in New York. I would appear as an anony-

3

mous girl eating a hamburger in Rose's Diner in "General Hospital," or as one-half of a nonspeaking young couple in a "Love of Life" nightclub scene. And when no roles were available I worked as a typist–file clerk in insurance offices, hardware stores, and small advertising agencies.

Every six months or so I either managed to fly back to Prairie Center, or my mother flew to New York. Always she brought me messages from people I'd grown up with, particularly young men. As time passed, though, the messages from young men grew fewer because most of them were engaged or married to girls I used to know.

A few still sent messages. The last time she was in New York my mother said, as we sat over dinner in my tiny apartment, "Bud Martin asked to be remembered to you."

"That's nice." Bud Martin's father owned the larger of Prairie Center's two drugstores.

"He also asked when you are coming home."

I said nothing.

"Bud is practically running the drugstore now. And there's talk that he'll buy out the Pates." Joe and Eileen Pates owned the other drugstore.

"I'm glad to hear Bud's doing so well."

"Catherine, I think you are the reason Bud hasn't married. I think he keeps hoping you'll come home." After a moment she added, in a soft voice, "So do I."

My heart twisted. I tried to smile into the blue-gray eyes almost the same shade as my own. "Mother, I've been in New York for more than five years. I don't belong in Prairie Center anymore. I think I never did. I belong here."

When she didn't answer I said, "I know I haven't got-

4

ten anyplace yet. But dammit, I've got talent. I'm still sure of it." When she still did not speak, I said, "Don't you think I have?"

She smiled and reached out to touch my hair. "Yes. And I guess you don't belong in Prairie Center. And I'm proud that you don't. But I miss you so."

"You don't have to miss me. Again and again I've asked you to move to New York. We could get a bigger apartment—"

She shook her head.

"Why not? It would be different if we had family there. But we haven't, not a soul."

That was the case. My mother, an only child, had been born late in the life of her parents. They had died soon after her marriage. When I was not quite two, the father I scarcely remembered had died, leaving my mother with enough money to open the small dress shop she still ran. While I was in grammar school a second cousin of my mother's still lived in Prairie Center, but more than fifteen years ago she and her husband had moved to California.

"With no relations there, why should you stay?"

My mother's voice was quiet. "I have friends there. And I have roots, roots that run more than fifty years deep." She paused long enough for me to remember that she was fifty-two. But her soft, pretty face did not look it, even though the hair that framed it, once almost the same dark blond shade as my own, was mostly gray now.

"I'm a small-town person, Catherine. I don't think I could survive in New York, any more than a tree could live down in the subway. But I do miss you. And besides—" She broke off, but I was almost certain what she wanted to talk about. Men.

After a moment she confirmed my guess. "Have you met anyone special lately?"

"No, Mother."

I had met just the usual. Business men who hired me as an office temporary, and who sometimes, whether or not they were married, made passes. Soap opera sound men and technicians whom I'd dated a few times. Actors who had asked me out, usually making clear that we were to go dutch on the evening's expenses.

"Do you still see Si Dalyrimple?"

"Yes."

Blond and good-looking and in his early thirties, with a perpetual suntan that came mostly out of a lamp, Si Dalyrimple was the nearest thing to a permanent fixture in my life. I had met him in a singles' bar my former roommates took me to soon after I came to New York. Since then, to my knowledge, he'd had three live-in girl-friends. I was the one he started telephoning whenever such arrangements broke up.

My mother said, "I like him very much."

No wonder. The last time she had been in New York Si had taken us to the Four Seasons and then to the Carlyle to hear Bobby Short. His manner to her had been a charming blend of diffidence and mild flirtatiousness. Before the evening was over she was glowing like a prom queen.

I said, "I like him too."

I did, except for the way he made the money he spent so freely. He financed some of the street peddlers you see all over Manhattan. Having advanced each peddler money to buy a stock of handbags or costume jewelry or toys, Si would collect half of their often handsome daily profits. Whenever one of his men was arrested for selling

6

merchandise without a license, Si would go down and pay the fine, after which his peddler would go back into business on another stretch of sidewalk.

Si was never arrested. Evidently backing peddlers financially was not against the law. And yet I felt there was something shabby about it. And I felt sorry for the legitimate shopkeepers struggling with taxes and licensing fees and utility bills and payrolls—only to look through their plate glass windows and see some peddler doing a land-office business in the same sort of merchandise they themselves offered.

Once when I made some tentative reference to those shopkeepers, Si laughed and said, "You've never been to Florence, have you?"

"You know I haven't."

"Well, if you had been, you'd have seen street peddlers on the Ponte Vecchio. In Venice you'd see them in the Piazza San Marco. And all over the Belleville section of Paris, Algerian peddlers spread out their oriental rugs and brass lamps and incense burners. Honey, I'm helping glamorize New York. Besides, people like those street stalls. If they didn't, they'd yell for a cop instead of buying."

Now my mother said tentatively, "Do you think that seeing Si might lead to something—definite?"

It might lead to something, all right, but probably not to the altar, as my mother obviously hoped. Rather it would lead to a renewed invitation to become live-in girlfriend number four. Or would it be five or six?

I said, "I don't know, Mother."

I took her to Kennedy the next morning and waited with her in the boarding lounge until the loudspeaker announced her plane's imminent departure.

I never saw her alive again. A month later she was hit by a car as she crossed the wide main street of that little Kansas town. My only comfort lay in the fact that she died instantly.

As I stood beside her open grave in a Prairie Center churchyard still patched with snow, I was surrounded by people I had known since childhood. I felt a sudden regret that I had not stayed here and married a local boy, and become like Marcella Baines Davis, who stood on the opposite side of the grave, her body swollen with what would be her third child. Her face, framed in a brown woolen scarf against the cold, had what I thought of as that several-years-a-housewife look—a little bored and resentful, but at least settled.

Yes, perhaps I should have followed Marcella's path. But it was too late now. Death had severed my last link to this town. Marcella and all these others realized it. I read questions in their eyes. What was I like by now, this girl who had left Prairie Center to become a famous actress, and who now appeared, every once in a while, as a background figure in some scene on their TV screen? How did she make out financially? Who were the men in her life?

And also each of these people had become a stranger to me, more of a stranger, say, than the boy at the checkout counter in the A & P near my apartment, with his here's-your-change-and-have-a-nice-day, even though it might be seven in the evening.

During the next few days, consultations with my mother's lawyer brought me at least some distraction from my grief, and my guilts, and my now useless regrets. The dress shop, I discovered, had not done well during the recent recession years, a fact my mother had concealed from me. To keep the place going, she had borrowed heavily from a local bank. The small house in which I had grown up was free and clear, but its sale under present market conditions would bring little more than enough to pay off the bank loan.

I left everything in the lawyer's hands and flew back to New York. Among the accumulated mail waiting for me was a letter from the two part-time actresses I had once lived with. They had leased a loft in the Soho district. They planned to live in the loft and, in a shop on the building's ground floor, offer "antique" clothing from the twenties through the fifties. If I could raise ten thousand dollars, I could come in with them.

"It's a great opportunity, Catherine, and not just because of what we'll make on the clothes. Play producers looking for authentic period costumes will come there, so you'd make lots of theater contacts."

No doubt. But I didn't have ten thousand dollars or any hope of acquiring such a sum soon.

I had returned to New York late in March. It was weeks later—just after the first warm spell in May, I think—that with appalling suddenness the city seemed to take on a new and sinister aspect. I don't know the reason for it. Could it have been a delayed reaction to my mother's death and to the realization of how alone I was? Perhaps. All I'm sure of is that subway graffiti no longer seemed to me amusing or even bearable. Instead, those orange suns with grinning faces, those exploding comets, those scrawled obscenities seemed to hold a threat. And other things I had once taken in my stride suddenly seemed intolerable. For instance, one of the writers of the soap opera which most often employed me had an active hatred of a cast member, an old character actor. It was an open secret that the writer was determined to have the old man "written out" of the script. I had tried not to let that disturb me. There was nothing I could do about it. And after all, how could I know but what there was a good reason for the writer's hostility?

But all of a sudden I could no longer blind myself to the cruelty of it. The little smile on the writer's lips when he walked onto the set to observe a rehearsal. The way the old man's hands would shake, and his voice stumble over his lines. I began to pray, whenever I was called by that particular soap, that the episode to be taped would not include the old man.

Other things happened that early summer. One night, dining alone in a booth in a fast-food restaurant on Columbus Avenue, I became aware of the conversation on the other side of the booth's high wall. A man was trying to rid himself of his wife. Perhaps earlier he had tried reasoned argument or cajolery. Now he was trying insults. Insults about her appearance, her age, the boredom she caused him.

Appalled, I stole a glance into the mirror behind the restaurant counter. I could see the pale-faced reflection of a woman of fifty-odd, her graying brown hair permanented into tight little curls. Rhinestones were set in the rims of her harlequin glasses. I could not see the man's face, just his large, meaty hand grasping a beer glass. I wanted to get up and walk out, but how would she feel, realizing that I must have heard the things he was saying?

"Haven't you got any self-respect, Doris? Why, if you came to me and said you wanted to marry someone else, I wouldn't try to hang onto you like some damn leech."

She sounded wretched, but she was still hanging in there. "You can't just walk out on me after thirty years.

How will I live?"

"I told you I'd pay seventy-five a week."

"Roy, you know the apartment rent is more than that."

"Then get some woman to share the rent with you. And get a job. Women are always yelling about being liberated. Well, here's your chance."

"A job? When I've got only a high school education and no experience? And when some people right out of college can't find jobs? You'll have to give me more than seventy-five a week, Roy."

"Greedy old bag, aren't you, Doris? Better watch it. Janis and I could just skip out of the state or even the country. Then where would you be?"

I pushed my unfinished dinner away from me, stood up, and walked out, not looking at the suddenly silent couple. I knew that such a conversation could have occurred almost anywhere, including Prairie Center. But as I stepped into the muggy air of Columbus Avenue, I thought, I'll bet it happens more often in New York.

That next week it seemed to me that the newspapers and the six o'clock news on TV recounted more than the usual number of murders, rapes, and arsonist-set apartment fires. Then on Friday, as I lunched at a hamburger stand near the wholesale furniture firm that had employed me all that week, I opened the early edition of the *New York Post*. On page three there was a photograph of the seal pool in Central Park with several small, sleek bodies floating in it. Sometime during the previous night a hunter had braved the wilds of Central Park to slaughter four seals.

It may sound shocking, but I think I would have felt less sickened if the gunman had shot four people. After all, people can choose to stay out of the park at night. The

11

seals lived there. I went back to my desk. I had been assigned to the sort of typing I dislike most—invoices with columns and columns of figures. But at least concentrating on those numbers kept me from thinking about the seals.

The next day, Saturday, Si Dalyrimple telephoned me. He had sent flowers for my mother's funeral, and after my return to New York he had taken me out a couple of times. But I hadn't heard from him for the past several weeks.

"How about a belated birthday dinner tomorrow night?"

"Whose birthday?"

"Yours. Didn't you have a birthday sometime this past week? What was it? Your twenty-fourth? Twenty-fifth?"

"Whatever."

As he knew very well, it had been my twenty-seventh. I had awakened that morning wondering if the muted rumble I heard was the subway or Time's Winged Chariot.

"If you're not busy that night, I thought we'd go to a new place on East Sixty-third. It's called Jean-Armand's. Have you heard of it?"

I had. Nouvelle cuisine served on enormous plates at even more enormous prices. Evidently the street-peddler business was doing well.

When we dined at Jean-Armand's on Sunday night, amid the almost religious hush you find in some of these places dedicated to gastronomic pleasures, I learned that the street-peddler business was indeed doing well. The police still hassled a few of his "boys" these days, but only occasionally was there an actual arrest. "And recessions are good for street merchants. Everyone wants bargains."

12

He took a forkful of Sole Jean-Armand and then said, "Maggie and I have split up."

The last time I had heard, he and Maggie, who shared an apartment near Lincoln Center, had been planning to rent a house in the Hamptons for the summer.

"It's definite?"

"Yes. She moved out three weeks ago. I didn't tell you about it then because—well, I thought you might feel better about it if I waited a while to ask you."

I didn't say, "Ask me what?" I already knew.

He said, "Well, how about it? It's damned lonely, living alone. And you know how I've always felt about you."

I remained silent, thinking.

I wasn't in love with Si. Furthermore, I felt uneasy about the way he made his living and about the sleazy cynicism I sometimes glimpsed beneath all that charm. But on the whole I liked him and found him attractive.

What was more, if I were ever to acquire that upwardly mobile husband, and house and child in Connecticut, I had best get cracking. And sometimes these live-in arrangements did lead to marriage. Quite often, in fact.

Then I realized I was kidding myself. Becoming Si's roommate could lead to only one thing. A year or so from now he would sit in some restaurant and say to some girl, "Catherine and I have split up."

I said, "Thank you, Si. But the answer is the same as last time."

For a moment I saw chagrin in that handsome face with the perpetual tan. Then he laughed and said, "Catherine, you don't really belong to the present. You belong back there in one of those June Allyson movies.

13

You know—a little white collar and a look that says, 'Don't touch me unless you've got an engagement ring in your pocket.' "

"Oh, Si! I'm not that bad."

"Of course you're not. And just to show you that there are no hard feelings, I shall pull out, not an engagement ring, but this."

He reached inside his pocket and then held out a folded piece of newsprint. "Maybe you didn't see this in the *Village Voice*. I know you don't read it regularly. If you'd agreed to move in with me, I'd never have shown it to you. But as it is—"

I unfolded the newsprint. It was part of an employment-offered column with one advertisement circled in red pencil:

"Actress in middle twenties sought for regional theater. Blonde preferred. Comparative unknown okay. Call one to four, afternoons." The telephone number that followed belonged to an East Side exchange.

I said slowly, "There's something strange about this ad. Usually they say to come to some theater for a tryout, or at least to some agent's office. And what does this mean, regional theater? Some sort of touring company?"

"It beats me."

"Maybe it's one of those apprentice deals. You pay *them* money, and they let you spend the summer taking tickets and painting scenery in some strawhat theater."

"Maybe. But if that's the deal, wouldn't they have advertised for a number of people, rather than just one girl?"

"I suppose so."

I reread the ad. "Middle twenties." Well, twenty-seven was still the middle twenties. "Blonde preferred." My hair was nearer blond than brown. "Comparative un-known okay." I certainly met *that* requirement.

I said, "One thing seems definite. The job's for some-thing out of town."

"I know. That's why I wouldn't have even shown it to you if you'd said yes to my little proposition. What have you got to lose?"

I felt an inward hesitation, almost an uneasiness. Then I thought of that little Kansas town where perhaps I had never fitted in, and certainly could not now. I thought of how disturbing, even sinister, once-glamorous New York now seemed to me.

Yes, indeed, what did I have to lose?

CHAPTER **2**

The fifth-floor corridor of the small but expensive East Side hotel was walnut paneled, newly carpeted, warmly lighted by amber globes set in brass wall sconces. I felt nervous as I pushed the bell of Room 5-E. But I also felt pleased and more than a little surprised that I had been summoned here.

Certainly my phone conversation the previous afternoon, with a woman who gave her name as Eunice Andexter, had not seemed promising. In an impersonal but pleasant voice with a New England accent she had asked my name, age, address, phone number, height, weight, and marital status.

Then: "What theatrical experience have you had, Miss Mayhew?"

There would have been no point in trying to gild the lily, even if I had wanted to. Such matters can be checked.

"In productions at my college I played Blanche DuBois

16

in *Streetcar* and Rosalind in *As You Like It*. Since I came to New York I've appeared in soap operas and in an off-off-Broadway play that flopped."

"Speaking parts in soap operas?"

"Only a line or two once in a while."

There was a silence. Well, I thought, that's that. The phrase "comparative unknown" evidently didn't apply to someone as unknown as I was.

Then she said, "I can't place your accent, Miss Mayhew. Where are you from?"

At least I had accomplished something during my six years in New York. With the aid of discs recorded by a voice teacher, I had managed to rid myself of my Midwestern twang and achieve the sort of regionless accent you hear on most TV radio broadcasts.

"I was born and raised in a small Kansas town."

For the first time she sounded a little impressed with me. "From your voice one would never know it." Then: "You must have found New York quite a contrast to where you grew up."

"Yes."

"Did your family approve of your coming here?"

A familiar twist of pain. "I didn't have any family except my mother. And now—" I broke off. No point in enlarging upon that. After a moment I added, "No, she didn't want me to come to New York, but neither did she stand in my way."

"I see. Well, only one question more. What is your coloration?"

"I have fair skin, grayish-blue eyes, dark blond hair. It's shoulder length, but I often wear it drawn into a knot at the back of my head."

"Well, thank you, Miss Mayhew. We may be in touch

17

with you." She hung up.

I still didn't know what her ad had meant by "regional theater." *What* region? But then, if I were not to be offered the job—and it looked as if I wouldn't be—what difference did it make?

The next morning, to my surprised delight, Miss Andexter phoned. Could I please come to the Hotel Briault, Room 5-E, at four that afternoon? Evidently something about me, perhaps the thoroughness with which I had shed my Midwestern accent, had interested her after all.

I phoned Office Temporaries. They get annoyed if you don't let them know when you won't be available. Then I dressed carefully in my best warm-weather outfit, a suit of heavy beige linen. I hesitated over my hair. Do it up into a knot for a cool, sophisticated look or let it hang loose and girlish? With no idea of the sort of role for which I would audition, I decided to let it hang.

Now, pushing the bell beside door 5-E, I heard soft chimes. After a moment the door opened. The man who stood there was slender and dark and perhaps forty, with a handsome, chiseled face that reminded me of someone. Almost instantly I realized who it was. He looked like Tyrone Power, the late film star, whose old movies keep running on TV.

Then I became aware that a certain startled expression had leaped into his dark eyes. Triumph? Pleasure? Some sort of recognition? It was gone before I could identify it.

"I'm Catherine Mayhew. Miss Andexter asked me to come here today."

"Oh, yes, Miss Mayhew. I recall your name from the list. My name is Dale Carling. Come in, please."

He opened the door wide, and I stepped into what apparently was the living room of a suite. It was filled with girls seated on two love seats lined up against the far wall, and armchairs, and straight chairs the hotel management must have drawn from some storeroom. The girls all had hair of varying shades of blond. All appeared to be under thirty, or at most under thirty-five. All were attractive, and three or four of them were so beautiful that my heart sank.

"Have a seat, please," Dale Carling said. He opened a door that I realized must lead to a bedroom and closed it quickly behind him.

I sank onto a straight chair. No one spoke to me, but everyone glanced at me, and a few gave me tentative smiles. Then they went back to reading, or staring at the walls, or, in the case of one glorious creature with lemon-colored hair and indigo eyes, to knitting a red muffler. I tried to cheer myself by recalling that the ad did not say applicants must be beautiful. And after all, there were roles—Maggie in *What Every Woman Knows*, for instance—that a raving beauty would be unable to play.

Time passed. Dale Carling reappeared frequently to usher a girl in or out of that inner room, or to admit some newcomer to the suite. The interviews in that bedroom—I'd caught enough glimpses of its interior to be sure it was a bedroom—were all brief. No one, not even the ravishing knitter, stayed in there more than five minutes.

At last it was my turn. Pulse beats rapid, I entered the bedroom with Dale Carling and heard him close the door behind us. Another man stood near the long windows on the opposite side of the room. Late afternoon light slanting through the glass showed me the armchairs upholstered in dark blue plush, the mahogany twin beds, and a mahogany desk pulled a few feet out from the wall.

A tall, slender woman rose from behind the desk and extended her hand. As I took it I saw in her hazel eyes much the same look I had glimpsed in Dale Carling's.

"It's nice to meet you, Miss Mayhew. I'm Eunice Andexter."

She was about fifty, a handsome fifty, with pepper-and-salt hair smartly cut and shaped, and regular features marred only by a slight heaviness in the jawline.

"I'm sure our friend Mr. Carling introduced himself. And this," she said, as the man across the room walked toward us, "is my brother, Brian Andexter."

Although he had the beginnings of a paunch, he appeared to be a few years younger than his sister, and his brown hair had no gray in it. But his features were similar to hers. In his case the somewhat heavy jaw was becoming.

"Please sit down, Miss Mayhew." His voice too had a New England accent.

I sat down in the armchair he held for me. The Andexters also sat. Dale Carling stood leaning against the wall beside the desk. I was aware of a tension in the air, and my hopes soared. For some reason, all three of them were interested in me.

Eunice Andexter said, "First of all, would you mind having your hair bleached to a lighter shade?"

"Not in the least."

"And you would have no objection to spending several weeks or months away from New York?"

"No."

"And there's no one to object if you do so?" She gave me a woman-to-woman smile. "No overpossessive boyfriend?"

"No." This time my voice was dry.

20

I intended to ask what role was to be played, and where, but before I could speak Miss Andexter said, "Could you tell us a little more about that off-off-Broadway play you were in?"

I did. After that Brian Andexter asked what work I'd done besides acting, and I told of some of my office temporary assignments. Then his sister asked several questions, including some she had asked over the phone the day before. Even Dale Carling, although the ringing of the doorbell kept him moving in and out of the room, managed to ask a question about my work in soap operas. I had the feeling that their real objective was not to gain answers but to spend more time observing me. Already this interview had lasted at least twice as long as that with any of those other girls. And that, surely, was a good omen.

At last I managed to get in a question of my own. "You implied that this job required leaving New York. Could you tell me just where—"

"Muskeegan, Maine."

"Oh!" I had never heard of Muskeegan nor of any drama companies in that part of the world, except for strawhat theaters in Bar Harbor. But that did not mean that there wasn't a group calling itself the Muskeegan Players or some such.

I asked, "And what particular role—"

"That has not been settled yet, not absolutely. But I can tell you the salary. It's eight hundred a week, with a twelve-week guarantee."

Eight hundred a week. Twelve times eight hundred was ninety-six hundred dollars, almost enough to take up my friends' offer of a share in their living loft and their dress shop.

21

I was sure now what these three were. Stagestruck amateurs, rich ones. I made a bet with myself that the play they would present would turn out to be the brainchild of one of them, or perhaps all three.

"I think we'll be calling you," Eunice Andexter said, "but right now we'll have to end this interview. Other girls have arrived, and it's only fair to see them."

Other girls certainly had arrived. At least seven or eight of them, including a willowy creature with Lauren Hutton cheekbones, now occupied the living room. But not even the cheekbones worried me. I felt sure that I was the one those three wanted.

CHAPTER **3**

WHEN I ENTERED my apartment late the next afternoon, after a feverishly exciting day spent typing an
insurance company payroll, my phone was ringing. I
snatched it up.

"Hello, Miss Mayhew. Dale Carling here. How about
dinner tonight?"

I blurted out, "Does that mean I've—"

"The part is yours if you want it."

If I wanted it!

"Anyway," he went on, "we can settle everything over
dinner. Do you like Chinese food?"

"Who doesn't?"

"Then how about meeting me at the Hunan Palace at
six-thirty? I know their food is pretty good."

I hesitated and then said, as tactfully as I knew how,
"It is, but I'm afraid that the place will be a little *too*
quiet at that hour." Perhaps he didn't know that in New
York no one but tourists from—well, Kansas, say—go to

dinner at six-thirty.

"Can't be helped. I have a business appointment later on this evening."

"Then I'd love to meet you at six-thirty."

The Hunan Palace, in the East Eighties, occupied the entire first floor of what had once been a warehouse. When I arrived at six-thirty, the vast place held at least three times as many waiters as customers. I said to the business-suited Chinese who greeted me, "I was to meet a Mr. Carling. Is he here yet?"

Apparently not long out of Hong Kong, he said, "You forro me, preeze."

He led me through subdued lighting past a long bar of red and gold lacquer, across a large room filled with empty tables, and then through a doorway in a trellis wall into another sea of empty tables. At sight of me, Dale Carling was getting up from a table in the far corner. Why had they placed him away back here, as if he, a man of movie-star good looks, bore the mark of some loathsome disease? Or had he himself chosen this isolated spot?

The waiter took our order for drinks—a martini for Dale Carling, white wine for me—and then went away. "You were certainly right about the place being dead." Then: "What is it?"

Across the room a man had gotten up from a table and was moving, back turned to me, toward the doorway in the trellised partition. His blond hair gleamed in the subdued light.

He'd gone through the doorway now. I said, "It was just that I thought I saw someone I know."

But in all probability it hadn't been Si Dalyrimple. In this light, and at that distance, one youngish blond man

24

would look much the same as another. Besides, Si ate at either staggeringly expensive places, like Lutece, or standing up at some midtown hot dog stand. And never, never would he have a restaurant meal before eight o'clock.

I said, "Please! Please tell me about the play—"

"The waiter's coming. Let's order our meal and enjoy our drink. Then we'll talk."

I checked an impulse to throw the small bowl of salted noodles on my side of the table into his face. He said, "Tell me about that small town in Kansas."

I shrugged. "There's nothing to tell. There must be thousands of towns like it."

"Eunice mentioned that you no longer have any family back in Kansas."

"There, or anywhere." I tried to speak matter-of-factly, fighting down the depression that always threatened to engulf me when I thought of my aloneness.

"Oh, come now. Everyone has somebody, at least a cousin."

"My mother had a cousin. She left Prairie Center with her husband when I was a small child. We heard she was remarried to someone out in California. I don't remember what her last name is now, if I ever knew it."

A waiter brought our won ton soup, withdrew. I said, "I can't wait any longer. Tell me. What is the play?"

Elbows propped on the table, he folded one slender hand over the other and looked at me with suddenly grave dark eyes.

"No play," he said.

After a stunned moment I echoed, "No play!"

"That's right. No play."

I said, with anger beginning to stir beneath my incredulity, "But there must be! You and the Andexters spoke of this theatrical group—"

"I know. But there isn't any theatrical group."

After a long moment I said bitterly, "Then just what sort of joke is this?"

"Believe me, it isn't a joke."

He was silent for several moments and then went on, "The Andexters very much needed someone like you. You see, they have an aunt, a desperately unhappy old woman with whom they've lived for many years, and whom they love very much. She's very ill with heart disease. In fact, her own doctor and a specialist he called in doubt that she will last through the summer. If it is humanly possible, Eunice and Brian want to make her last months of life happy ones."

"How very touching," I said, feeling not in the least touched. "But what has all that to do with me?"

"You look very much like the granddaughter whose disappearance made Josephine Andexter so miserable. Or anyway, you look the way Karen must look now after a lapse of eight years. It was in hope of finding someone like you that the Andexters came down here, although their aunt thinks they are just on their annual shopping trip."

I thought of the look of discovery that had leaped into Dale Carling's eyes when he first saw me standing in that hotel corridor. Later I'd seen the same expression on Eunice and Brian Andexter's faces.

Now he said, "Don't you want to hear about it?"

I merely looked at him, narrow-eyed. He said, "There's still a job, you know. Eight hundred a week plus room and board for spending the summer in Maine."

Maine. Cool woodland instead of asphalt so hot that,

with your heel stuck in it, you sometimes literally walked out of your shoe. The seethe of waves on a rocky beach rather than the shriek of sirens and the high-pitched whine of garbage truck compactors in the predawn hours.

And, a few weeks from now, nearly ten thousand extra dollars in the bank.

I said, still sullenly distrustful, "All right. Tell me."

After a moment he said, "There *is* a town of Muskeegan. Josephine Andexter's house is about five miles from it. She inherited the place from her husband, John Andexter, who died in the nineteen-thirties. John's father had built the house back in the eighteen-seventies from money made out of lumber and shipping. I imagine people back then must have called the place Andexter's Folly, a house built away off in the woods when he could have built it in the richest section of Augusta. But then, there is a strain of eccentricity in the Andexters."

I said, still sullen, "What do you mean, eccentricity?"

"Just that. Shall I go on?"

Resentful, but lured by the thought of pine forests and crashing surf and money in the bank, I nodded.

"John Andexter married Josephine in nineteen-twenty, and brought her to Pinehaven."

"Pinehaven?"

"The not very original name of the Andexter house. It was John's second marriage. He was more than twice Josephine's age. His first marriage had produced no children, and for a while it looked as if Josephine too would remain childless. But in nineteen-twenty-five her son Michael was born. She adored him, of course, especially after her husband died. Michael was about three then."

All through our Hunan chicken with snow peas, and Chinese beef with mushrooms, and several cups of tea, Dale went on talking. When Michael was twenty-one, Dale told me, he had married a girl who had worked as a stenographer in the town where he had attended college. Josephine had never met the girl until Michael brought her to Pinehaven as a bride. No doubt she had been disturbed by her son marrying so young. But probably all had been forgiven when, less than a year later, Josephine's granddaughter Karen was born.

"But the baby's mother lived less than a week after the birth," Dale said. "And when Karen was three, her father Michael crashed his sport car on a mountain road and died in the wreckage."

I said, "And Josephine and her little granddaughter went on living in that house?" By then I had begun to visualize it, a white frame house of many cupolas and bay windows set incongruously in pine woods.

Dale nodded. "Except for the servants, they had lived alone there until Eunice and Brian came to stay with their Aunt Josephine fifteen years ago. Little Karen was almost twelve then. Eunice and Brian were of course long since grown up."

I frowned. "Since their name is Andexter, they must be the niece and nephew of Josephine's husband, John Andexter."

"That's right. Their father was Benjamin Andexter, John's younger brother. He and his wife died years and years ago, when Eunice and Brian were barely out of their teens."

There had been a certain constraint in his voice. It prompted me to ask, "And neither Eunice nor Brian has ever married?"

28

"No."

"Why not?"

"I have no idea. Anyway, isn't that rather off the subject?" Meaning that it was none of my business.

"I suppose so. But do you mind telling me why they came to live with their Aunt Josephine fifteen years ago?"

"Not through any financial necessity. They'd lived fairly comfortably for years and years in Bangor, off money left them by their parents, plus whatever sums their work brought them."

"Work?"

"They are both artists. Eunice paints and Brian sculpts. Neither of them is at all well known. But they do make sales every once in a while."

"You haven't yet told me why they came to live with their aunt."

"They're very fond of her. They have been ever since, as teenagers, they spent several summers with their Aunt Josephine and their cousin Michael. They felt especially close to her after Michael died in that car crash, leaving her with no one except a granddaughter who was scarcely more than an infant.

"Fifteen years ago Josephine confessed to Eunice and Brian that she just couldn't cope any longer. Not with the house, or the servants, or financial matters. Much as they hated to leave their friends and a life they were used to in Bangor, they finally decided they must. They listed their house with a real estate agent and moved into Pinehaven. As I believe I said, Karen was not quite twelve then."

Karen, the girl whose disappearance eight years ago had made her grandmother so wretched. I said, "How old was Karen when she disappeared?"

"Eighteen. She just left a note for her grandmother,

saying that she needed to go away and that her grandmother was not to worry. Not worry!" He shook his head
disgustedly. "Well, maybe at eighteen a girl can't realize
what cruelty she is inflicting upon a parent or grand-
parent who adores her. Anyway, she just vanished."

"Surely her grandmother and the Andexters tried to
find her."

"Of course. Advertisements, detectives, everything.
They never traced her farther than Augusta, Maine,
where she left her car in a parking lot—the attendant
remembered her—and then took a plane, or a bus, or
even thumbed her way to God knows where."

A few more diners had arrived now, but the maitre d'
had placed none of them near us. I felt sure Dale Carling
had tipped him to leave the neighboring tables vacant. I
could understand that now. He could never have talked
so freely within earshot of other diners.

I said evenly, "And you want me to try to convince this
sick old lady that her beloved granddaughter has come
back to her."

His voice was calm. "Exactly. It would be a deception,
but a merciful one."

"It would be an impossible one. Perhaps my appearance would fool her, especially if I bleached my hair.
That's why Eunice Andexter wants me to bleach it, isn't
it?" He nodded. "But my voice! Surely my voice isn't like
Karen's."

"I know three answers to that objection. First, can *you*
hear in your mind's ear the exact intonations of a voice
you haven't heard for eight years? Second, Josephine Andexter no longer hears well. Third, you obviously are
good at discarding and adopting accents. The Andexters
brought with them a record of Karen's voice. When she

30

was sixteen she wrote a poem for her grandmother's birthday and recorded it. I'm sure that after you've played it a number of times you'll be able to pick up not only the way down-easters flatten their vowels but also her individual intonations."

For the first time, I realized that he, unlike the Andexters, had not even a trace of Maine accent. "You're not a down-easter yourself?"

"No. I was raised in Connecticut. Later I moved to Bangor. That's when I met Eunice and Brian." Whether to ward off questions about himself or to return as swiftly as possible to the main topic, he said, "Well, will you do it?"

"It just wouldn't work. Even if I did manage to fool Mrs. Andexter, how about the servants? And the people in the town? What was its name?"

"Muskeegan. As for the servants, there are only four full-time ones. Servants are hard to get these days, no matter how much you are willing to pay. And of the four, only Mabel Brill, the housekeeper, was there eight years ago. The others are all comparatively new. And the townspeople will accept you as Karen. Why shouldn't they? You're about the right age. And believe me, Catherine, you look so much like Karen—or rather, the way she must look by now—that you could almost be her twin."

Doubtful and obscurely frightened and yet fascinated, I began to feel that it just might work. Except—

"What could I tell my—What could I tell Karen's grandmother about how I've spent the past eight years?"

"You can't tell her. You can't remember. You came to in Manhattan with no memory of how you got here. You couldn't even remember when and how you left Pine-

31

haven. You only knew that you lived there the first eighteen years of your life."

"Oh, lord! Not *amnesia*." In every soap in which I have appeared, sooner or later some character has suffered amnesia.

"Why not? It happens. And not just in soap operas," he added, almost as if he had read my mind. "Isn't it better than trying to make up a story about where you've been from the age of eighteen to twenty-six? Josephine Andexter will be so glad to see you that she'll accept any story. And besides—" He broke off.

"Besides what?"

"As I mentioned, there's an eccentric streak in the Andexters. She'll easily believe such a thing could have happened to you. As for other people, you can refuse to discuss your amnesia with them. After all, what business is it of theirs?"

And what business of yours, I wanted to say, are the Andexters? But I didn't want to put it that rudely. After all, I was still tempted by those pine woods and that eight hundred a week. And if they decided I might prove too difficult to handle they might perhaps try to find another girl.

And so instead I asked, "Would you mind telling me what your relationship with the Andexters is?"

"Brian and Eunice are my friends, my best friends. In fact, I've been living with them at Pinehaven for more than six months now."

"You can do that? Just drop everything and be someone's house guest for six months at a time?"

He smiled. "Are you asking if I'm rich? I'm not. I have an insurance agency in Bangor. Fortunately, I also have a capable assistant. He's been running the business for the last six months. I'd be making more if I were tending the store, all right. But I get by. And Brian and Eunice needed me."

Evidently they did, or at least thought they did. They had even entrusted to him the task of explaining what they really wanted of me. Why was that? Did they think that he, with his good looks and practiced salesmanship, would be more persuasive?

I said, "And you don't have anything except business ties to keep you from leaving Bangor whenever you choose to?"

Again he smiled. "Like a wife, for instance? No, I'm not married. And I'm not going to give the usual coy explanation that I've never found a girl who would have me. The truth is that I find the world too full of attractive women like yourself for me to settle for just one." He added swiftly, "I mean that as a compliment. I hope you didn't think it was also a pass."

I hadn't. I somehow sensed that I did not hold that sort of attraction for him. Nor did I find him physically attractive, despite those dark good looks. The chemistry was wrong, somehow.

I said, "And after Josephine Andexter's death, what does her supposed granddaughter do then?"

"As far as the townspeople are concerned, she'll go away on a trip, quite openly this time, and then just decide not to come back. In reality, you'll come back here with a nice little nest egg you didn't have when you left."

The waiter served us a dessert of preserved kumquats. When he had gone away, Dale said, "Well? Will you do it?"

I sat silent. I had a feeling that there was something hidden, something wrong, about the Andexters' propo-

33

sition. But I could not fathom what it might be. With an inward smile I reflected that they certainly could not be white slavers, like the Rossiters in that new soap "Lest Fall the Night." White slavers could pick up any number of girls younger than I—and dumber—from among those arriving each day at the Port Authority bus station.

Nor could the Andexters hope to use me in some scheme to extract money from their aged aunt. Karen, missing for eight years, probably could be declared legally dead, thus leaving Eunice and Brian as Josephine Andexter's closest relatives and legitimate heirs. All they would have to do would be to wait to inherit.

Dale said, "From your silence I gather that you need more time to make up your mind."

I nodded.

"Very well. I'll call you tomorrow."

"I just remembered something. Before you told me why the Andexters really wanted to hire me, you made sure that I had no relatives, no lover—"

"Of course. If you're to be Karen Andexter, Brian and Eunice can scarcely risk having some cousin or lovesick boyfriend showing up to tell their aunt that you're not. Would you like a brandy or something? No? Then shall we go?"

We moved back through the tables, at least half of them filled now. Out on Eighty-sixth Street I saw that twilight had descended upon the broad sidewalk and upon the crowd, slower paced than in the daytime, that moved past the cut-rate drugstores and shoe shops and German-styled beer halls. Dale looked at his gold-banded watch.

"Fifteen after eight, and I'm supposed to meet someone

at the Ambassador at eight-thirty. But right now I'll put you in a cab."

"No need. I can take the subway."

"No, you can't. If I'm to call you in the morning, I want you to get home safely tonight."

Quite a few cabs were cruising, now that the theater rush was about over. One slid to the curb in answer to Dale's signal. He opened the door for me, then handed the driver a bill and gave him my address. That startled me until I recalled that I had given my address as well as my phone number to the Andexters.

The cab moved south on Lexington. Soon traffic began to slow as cars and trucks turned onto the avenue from the sidestreets. Finally my cab halted, one of a line of cars and trucks blocking the intersection and the crosswalk.

I looked at the crowd of pedestrians on the nearest corner. Among them, swaying slightly, was a tall man of about thirty with lanky dark hair and a silly smile. The smile made the blood running down the side of his face from some sort of scalp wound seem all the more shocking. People around him kept stealing glances at him and then looking away.

The line of cars moved slowly forward. After a moment I said to the cab driver, "Did you see that man back there, the one who'd been—hurt?"

"Yeah. From the look of him he was high on something, too."

I did not say, "No one was helping him." I knew that if I did the driver would say something like, "Can't blame them. For all they knew, the guy who slashed him might be right there in the crowd, ready to knife anybody who seemed to be getting nosy."

I thought, I've got to get away from here, at least for a while.

Shafts of light angling through pine trees onto a needle-strewn path. Leaps of squirrels from branch to branch. Air in which evergreen scents mingled with the salty tang of the sea.

I was going to take up the Andexters' offer.

CHAPTER 4

O<small>N AN AFTERNOON</small> more than a week later, an elderly
man in a chauffeur's uniform a little large for his thin
frame met us at the airport near Muskeegan, Maine. It
was a small airport, with a short landing strip suitable
only for the sort of old prop plane to which we had
transferred in Augusta. Brian Andexter and Dale Carling
and the aged chauffeur, who had been introduced to me
as Hazzard, carried our luggage to the car in the almost
empty parking lot, an old but obviously well-kept
Bentley.

With Dale riding up front beside Hazzard and Eunice
and Brian and me riding in back, the car traveled along a
wide dirt road. Through the anxiety that gripped me I
was aware that this was not the sort of Maine landscape I
had been visualizing this past week. Rather, it was a
rural slum. Sizable stumps indicated that once the area
had been a fully grown forest, but now only second- or
third-growth pines were left. Shacks sat in small

37

clearings, most of them with at least two wrecked cars in their dooryards. Children playing among the wrecks and the tire swings hung from pine branches stopped to stare at us as we passed.

But I was only dimly conscious of my surroundings. Most of my attention was centered on my conviction that I was about to fail. True, I had seen, not suspicion, but mere curiosity in the old chauffeur's eyes when Eunice had said, "Hazzard, this is our cousin, Miss Karen Andexter." For a moment I had a relieved sense of having passed the first test. Then I recalled Eunice telling me that, despite his age, the present Andexter chauffeur was not an old family retainer, someone who could remember the long-missing granddaughter. He had been hired only five years ago to replace another driver, a distant relative of his, who had suffered a heart attack.

We entered Muskeegan's main street, a street so wide that cars parked at angles to the curb. It appeared to be a fairly large town, with three banks, two drugstores, a large grocery store whose sign identified it as Mason's Superette, and several bars. But many of the shops were empty with for-rent signs in their plate glass windows. Eunice—or perhaps it was her brother—told me that the town had been in a depressed state ever since a local lumber mill had dismissed about half of its employees several years before.

Nearly all of the people moving along the sidewalks glanced at least briefly at the chauffeur-driven car. A few waved, and Brian and Eunice returned the waves. I doubt if any of those pedestrians got a clear look at me, seated between the Andexters.

The car left the town. Soon we were moving through the sort of forest I had visualized, towering pines that

38

shadowed the entire road. We were now on Aunt Josephine's land, Eunice said. Just as she had throughout the journey, from vast and echoing La Guardia Airport to this pine-bordered road, she went on chatting in her calmly pleasant voice. Those pink flowers in a natural clearing we had just passed, she told me, were wild geraniums. And those small birds who scratched chicken-fashion under the trees at the road's edge were eastern towhees. From her manner one would never have suspected how she and I and the two men had spent that last hectic week in New York.

Or at least for me it had seemed hectic. I had sent my landlord written notice that I was giving up the shabbily furnished cubbyhole he called an apartment. No point in paying rent all summer when, in the fall, I would be moving into the loft above the dress shop. Not that I had told my former roommates that I would be taking up their offer. That would have meant explaining how I planned to obtain close to ten thousand dollars within a few weeks. And I did not want to tell anybody that. I did not want to run even the remote risk that curiosity would lead my ex-roommates, or Si, or anyone else to come up to Muskeegan to see how I was making out in my role as Karen Andexter.

During that week I'd had my hair lightened at a beauty salon. And I had spent hours listening to Karen Andexter's recorded "poem," an atrocious and yet touching rhyme that she had written, at the age of sixteen, as a present for her grandmother's birthday. Before long not only the Andexters and Dale Carling but even I felt that I could pass for a girl who, except for a few semesters at a private school in Connecticut, had spent all of her early years in Maine. And before the week was out I felt that I had mastered the intonations of that particular sixteen-year-old's voice grown a decade older.

"And anyway," Eunice pointed out, "no one at Pine-haven will be in the least interested in proving you are *not* Karen. Aunt Jo will be overjoyed to accept you, and it won't matter one way or another to the servants. Besides, as we've already told you, the only servant who has been there long enough to remember Karen is the housekeeper, Mrs. Brill."

Midway in that hectic week the Andexters and I had dinner—carryout chicken paprika from a nearby Hungarian restaurant—in my apartment. Dale was not there. He'd flown to Bangor on business connected with his insurance agency and wouldn't be back until just before we all flew up to Maine. After dinner Brian drew for me a sketch of Pinehaven's interior and the grounds surrounding it. Then he looked at his sister with his usual pleasantly bland expression. "You're going to phone Mrs. Brill to get Karen's old room ready for her, aren't you?"

She nodded her smartly coiffed head.

He looked back at me. "Karen's old room is exactly as she left it. Aunt Jo wouldn't allow it to be altered in any way."

"Brian, why don't you say *your* old room," Eunice cut in. She turned to me. "You'll find the situation more comfortable if, as much as possible, you think of yourself as Karen."

"All right," Brian said amiably. "*Your* old room hasn't been changed. There have been a few minor changes elsewhere over the years, of course, but I don't think anyone would expect you to remember that the wallpaper in the breakfast room used to have another pattern, or that

40

paintings in the library have been switched around."

Now, as the Bentley turned a curve in the road, Eunice reached over and grasped my hand. Her voice was no longer calm, but serious and urgent. "We'll be there soon. Now remember. You won't have to say much this afternoon. We've already told Aunt Jo all that she'll need or want to know."

All that she'd need or want to know. And all of it a lie. A lie about how Eunice and Brian, in New York on their ostensible shopping trip, had heard a news broadcast concerning a girl who had walked into a Manhattan police station and said that her name was Karen Andexter and that she had no idea how she had gotten to New York. She only knew that sometime in the past she had left her grandmother's house in Maine, for reasons she could not remember.

Eunice and her brother and Dale Carling had even thought of a way to keep Josephine Andexter from probing for those lost memories. Over the phone they had told her that they had taken her granddaughter to a psychiatrist, and that in his opinion any attempt to force her to remember might be disastrous to her mental equilibrium. Unless she spontaneously recalled the events of those lost eight years, it would be better to leave them shrouded forever.

As had happened more than once this past week, I felt a stab of guilt. But there was no reason to feel it. I wasn't hurting anyone. Quite the contrary. By taking part in this deception I would bring peace and happiness to what was left of a grief-tormented woman's life.

The Bentley moved around a curve. And there before

41

us was the house, set back on its huge oval of lawn. It was not the white frame Victorian of my imaginings. Instead it was something even more incongruous in this pinewood setting, a large, many-turreted brownstone of the sort rich men built in the past century, usually on a hill overlooking whatever town it was from which they had extracted their wealth. All that was missing was a herd of iron deer on the lawn.

Why on earth should Karen Andexter's great-grandfather have chosen to build a town-style mansion in these woods? There must indeed have been an eccentric streak in the Andexter blood.

A graveled drive curved around the lawn, passing the fan-shaped steps that led up to a flagstone terrace. Beyond the steps another drive led around the turreted corner of the house toward the rear. When the Bentley stopped in front of the steps, Brian said to his sister, "You two go on in. Dale and I will help Hazzard carry in the luggage."

Heart pounding, I accompanied Eunice Andexter up the steps to the double front doors, etched glass ones protected by wrought iron grilles. The doors opened before we reached them. A small, plump woman of about sixty stood just beyond the threshold. Arm around my waist, Eunice drew me into the entrance hall. I had an impression of a hardwood floor with small oriental rugs scattered over its gleaming surface. A broad staircase with a banister of heavy dark wood rose up to a shadowy landing. From somewhere beyond the foot of the stairs came the stately ticking of a grandfather's clock.

Eunice said, "Hello, Mrs. Brill." Then, with that protective arm around me: "Well, here she is. Our little

42

Karen, come back to us."

"So I see."

The tone was dry. The plump face was expressionless except for the eyes. Small and gray, they looked at me with undisguised hostility.

My heart plummeted. The woman had recognized me immediately as an impostor. Even before I had met Josephine Andexter, the whole plan had collapsed. No summer in Maine, no eight hundred a week, no part interest in the dress shop. And no happy last days for a sick old woman.

The housekeeper said, "You said over the phone you wanted me to get her old room ready for her."

"That's right. I'll wait down here until the men bring in the luggage." If Eunice was aware of Mrs. Brill's hostility, her serene voice did not indicate it. Perhaps, I thought, with a surge of hope, the woman was always sour-mannered.

"Better I show you the way," she said to me, "in case you've forgotten."

Unmistakable sarcasm in her voice. Again I was sure that she had seen right through me.

I followed her plump figure up to the landing. She led me to the left, past the grilled gate of a small elevator, and then opened a door. The bedroom beyond was large and attractive, although it struck me as a bit girlish even for an eighteen-year-old. Ivory wallpaper scattered with violet nosegays. Cherrywood chest of drawers and small desk and tall wardrobe. Four-poster bed with a blue canopy. Beneath the wide windows, which faced toward the front lawn, there was a long window seat cushioned in the same blue. In the righthand wall a half-opened

43

door gave me a partial view of a bathroom.

"I put sheets and blankets on the bed after Miss Eunice's phone call," the housekeeper said. "The bed had been stripped. Otherwise it was left the same for eight years. Those were Mrs. Andexter's orders."

She turned and faced me, hands on hips in the classic pose of contempt. While the pulse pounded in the hollow of my throat, she said, "But don't think that you fool me for one minute, missy. Amnesia, my foot!"

Unable to think of a reply, I stood silent.

"You just don't want to have to tell what you've been up to these past eight years, that's all. And God knows you've probably got good reason not to tell."

While I stood numb, she went on, "You were all right as a child. A mite spoiled, but so pretty and winning that nobody could hold it against you. You were even nice enough as a young girl. At least you always seemed to love your grandmother.

"But something happened to you at that school you went to in Connecticut, didn't it? You got into bad company or something. Anyway, it changed you."

When I just looked at her, she went on, "Well, I don't expect you to talk to me about it. But one thing I do know. You told your cousins and those New York policemen that you don't remember leaving Pinewood. But you still remembered leaving when you wrote that letter from Scranton two weeks afterward, didn't you?

"Oh, yes!" she said triumphantly. "I was the one who sorted the mail that day. I didn't give your letter to your grandmother because I was afraid it might be exactly the sort of letter it was, mean and vicious and wicked. You'd broken her heart when you ran off. Why did you have to write a letter that would have tormented her even more?

I've still got that letter, but I haven't shown it to your cousins or to anyone for fear they might mention it to your grandmother."

I stood silent.

She looked me up and down. "You'd think it would show in your face, the things you must have been doing. But it doesn't. You look older, but that's about all. Well, I guess the devil takes care of his own."

Turning toward the door she said, in a more neutral tone, "Dinner's still at seven, but that leaves you plenty of time to see your grandmother."

She went out. Relief left me so weak that I walked over to the window seat and sank down on it. To put it mildly, the woman disliked me. But at least she seemed to have no doubt that I was Karen.

Until she went away to that Connecticut school, Mrs. Brill said, Karen had seemed to love her grandmother. Certainly that "poem" she had recorded for her grandmother's birthday, with its forced rhymes and ragged meter, had seemed to hold love. I thought of its opening lines:

> Maybe I didn't always mind,
> But you were always, always kind.
> Maybe sometimes I was downright bad
> And made you awfully, awfully sad.
> But I swear to you, Nana, by stars above
> You'll forever have my love

A number of lines later the rhyme ended:

> And so in my heart there's a banner unfurled
> That says you're the best Nana in all the world.

And yet a little more than two years later she had run off, leaving a note on that dressing table over there, a note that said merely that she "couldn't" stay at Pinewood any longer and that her grandmother was "not to worry."

I walked over to the dressing table, which was skirted in that same blue material, and looked at the pictures on its glass-topped surface. A framed snapshot of a young couple, neither of them more than twenty-one or -two, standing beside a red MG. Karen's parents, sometime before her birth? Probably. And that sport car might have been the one in which he eventually had crashed, leaving his small daughter fatherless as well as motherless.

There were a number of pictures that, I soon realized, were of the same woman, taken at different periods of her life. Was she Josephine Andexter? Almost certainly. And the very number of pictures indicated that Karen indeed loved her grandmother. What was apparently the earliest snapshot showed a strawhatted man and a much younger woman on a ship's deck, he in white flannels, she in a cloche hat and long-waisted, short-skirted dress. John and Josephine Andexter on their wedding trip? Perhaps. There was a formal portrait of what appeared to be the same woman at about the age of forty. A snapshot apparently taken some years later showed her with a little blond girl on her lap. Her granddaughter Karen, almost certainly. And finally there was another silver-framed formal portrait, probably made not long before Karen disappeared, that showed Josephine Andexter as white-haired, serene-faced, smiling.

But the picture that interested me most was a color snapshot of Eunice and Brian Andexter seated on the front steps of this house with a young girl sitting between them. The girl looked so much like the picture of me in my high school yearbook that we might have been twins. According to the old saying, everyone has a double somewhere in the world. Here was a snapshot of mine.

Someone knocked. Dale Carling's voice said, "Karen?"

I opened the door. He came in, set down the oversized suitcase I had bought in New York, and then made the sort of congratulatory gesture—thumb and forefinger forming an oval—that managers flash from the wings in old movie musicals.

"You can get past anyone if you can get past Brill. And you did. I just talked to her downstairs."

"I know. Although for a while there I was sure she had seen right through me." I broke off and then said, "It seems she disapproved of Karen, not just because of her running away, but for the way she'd been behaving even before that."

"The way *you'd* been behaving. Try to think of yourself that way."

"All right. I'll try."

"Karen—I mean you—did start to change around the age of sixteen."

"Do you have any idea why? Mrs. Brill mentioned something about getting into bad company at that Connecticut school."

He shrugged. "Could have been. Or it could have been some other reason. Or just the way kids do change around that age. Anyway, I wouldn't know."

I had a distinct feeling that not only he, but Eunice and Brian also, knew a lot more about Karen than they had told me so far. It was the sense of being deceived that made me decide not to mention the letter Mrs. Brill had told me about. I wouldn't mention it to anyone, at least not until I had a better idea of whatever emotional un-

47

dercurrents, past and present, swept through this incongruously urban looking house set out here in the pine forest.

Dale said, "Eunice will come here in a few minutes to take you to your grandmother's room. She suggests you wear that dress you and she bought at Bloomingdale's last week."

I nodded. A simple shirtmaker, it was made of lavender linen. Lavender had been Karen's favorite shade for clothing.

"Well, see you at dinner," Dale said, and went out.

I took a quick shower. The modern showerhead was quite a contrast to the rest of the bathroom, with its massive marble tub, marble basin, and pull-chain toilet. I was dressed in the lavender shirtmaker when Eunice knocked.

She inspected me for several seconds and then said, "You look exactly right." Her tone still held that pleasant calm, but nevertheless I could tell that she, like me, felt blended hope and anxiety.

We went out into the wide corridor, turned right. I asked in a low voice, "Is your room in this wing?"

"No. Only yours and Aunt Jo's."

She halted, knocked lightly on a door, opened it. We stepped into a room.

"Well, Aunt Jo, here she is."

Josephine Andexter sat across the room in a rattan-sided wheelchair. Later I realized that she, wanting to appear her best for her granddaughter, must have dressed for this occasion as carefully as I had. Her knitted two-piece dress, with its exquisitely scalloped neckline, was of shell pink. She wore two strands of pearls. Light from the window behind her shone through the carefully arranged

48

white curls that framed her face. It was an old face, as finely wrinkled as a white kid glove. But the blue eyes, alight with tenderness and joy, looked young.

My throat tightened up. For the first time I realized what these past eight years must have been like for her. The helpless bewilderment. The grief. The agonized speculations about her granddaughter's fate.

I no longer felt a vague guilt about coming here, only gladness. It was I who had brought that joy into her face.

"Karen! My little Karen!" She held out narrow hands to me, hands that shook.

Suddenly I felt almost as if I *were* Karen. I felt a tenderness for her, much as I had felt for my mother, who was beyond reach of my tenderness now. Before I was aware of what I intended to do, I moved quickly across the room, sank to the carpet, and put my head in her lap.

I felt her trembling hand caress my hair. "It is all right, my darling. No one is going to ask you questions, or trouble you in any way. You're home now, and that is all that counts."

CHAPTER 5

At first I did not know when it was that the strange sound in my room awoke me. Then I reached for the luminous-dialed wristwatch I had placed on the stand beside the canopied bed. Eight minutes after two.

Until that moment, I had slept soundly, despite the strangeness of my surroundings. Perhaps that was because the evening had passed so peacefully.

Although according to her niece, Josephine Andexter usually took her meals in her room, she'd had dinner with all of us that night. Brought down in the small elevator by her nephew and wheeled into the dining room, she presided at the head of the table, her finely wrinkled face aglow with happiness. She ate very little of her chicken tarragon and broccoli. When Eunice urged her to eat, she answered, "I'm too excited!" But she did drink a glass of sauterne.

The food was excellent. When I made some comment about it, Mrs. Andexter said, "I'm so glad you like Hannah's cooking, my darling. She's been with us two years now. Or is it three?"

"Almost four," Brian said.

"As long as that? Anyway, we were lucky to get her."

Mrs. Brill served the meal. Her face was expressionless most of the time, but when she spoke to Mrs. Andexter, both her face and her voice softened. Obviously she was devoted to her employer.

After the dessert of lemon mousse, Mrs. Andexter said, "My dears, I don't think I'll have coffee with you. I'm getting rather tired." She smiled at me. "Come kiss me, Karen."

That afternoon it had been a spontaneous emotion that had sent me across the room to her. But now I felt very conscious of the gaze of three pairs of eyes as I left my place, went to the end of the table, and bent to kiss her soft cheek.

Brian wheeled her away and then returned to join us for coffee. It was served, not in the living room across the broad front hall from the dining room, but in the library. Eunice had told me that the living room seldom was used, and after a glimpse of it, a vast room filled with richly brocaded but uncomfortable-looking chairs and sofas, I could understand why. But the library, which adjoined the dining room, was pleasant. A fire in the grate, unnecessary on this early June evening but pleasant to look at, sent wavering light over the book-lined walls and the mahogany cabinet of a large TV set. While we watched a broadcast of area news from Augusta, Eunice poured small cups of coffee from the service Mrs. Brill had placed before her.

After a while Eunice leaned toward me. "You liked her from the first moment, didn't you?"

She said it very softly, under cover of the sound from the TV set, but I was surprised that she had said it at all, here where Mrs. Brill might walk into the room at any moment. Before we left New York the Andexters and Dale had impressed upon me that we should all guard our tongues. A few careless words, overheard by one of the servants and repeated to Mrs. Andexter, might shatter the joyous illusion they had worked so hard to create for her.

I said, also in a low voice, "Yes. The moment I saw her, she seemed so—appealing."

Eunice smiled. "She has always been so."

When the news was over, Eunice suggested that we go to our rooms. I welcomed the idea. The many hours of travel, from New York to Augusta to Muskeegan to this old house, had finally caught up with me, and I felt exhausted.

In my darkened room I had lain awake for only a few minutes, thinking of that other girl who once had occupied this bed. Then dreamless sleep closed down on me, and I knew nothing until I was awakened by that strange sound.

More puzzled than alarmed, I lay very still. It was a soft mournful sound, something between a child's whimper and the cry of some small animal—a cat, say. I switched on the bedside lamp. Although the sound continued, I saw nothing, no one, just the pretty furniture, the violet-nosegay wallpaper, the dressing table covered with photographs of the once-loved grandmother Karen had treated so brutally.

I got out of bed and, barefooted, looked into the closet where I had hung my clothes and then into the bathroom. The sound had ceased now. Perhaps it had been a cat out in the hall, even though the soft wailing had seemed to come from within this room.

I got back into bed, turned off the light. I had not even begun to settle down for sleep when that soft crying started again. This time I did not turn on the light. I got out of bed, went to the door, looked out into the hall. It stretched emptily away in both directions, illuminated only by the few widely spaced amber wall lights that had been left burning.

Then movement caught my eye. Perhaps twenty yards down the hall, on the opposite side of the stair landing, a door opened. Dale Carling, in a dark dressing gown, moved out into the hall and then turned around. On the room's threshold, out of my sight except for her profile and for her bare arms encircling his neck, Eunice lifted her lips for his kiss.

I drew back into my room and closed the door softly. With only a trace of chagrin I realized that even though the movie-star handsome Dale had made it clear he was not attracted to me, he apparently was not averse to sharing Eunice Andexter's bed. Well, some men preferred older women. Anyway, it was none of my business.

The crying noise had ceased, but it began again before I had moved halfway across the room. A sudden thought made me go to the window and look out. Of course! A wind. Across the broad lawn I could see the tops of pine trees in motion against a sky washed by the light of a waning half moon. As I watched, the motion ceased. An instant or two later, so did the crying.

Often wind sweeping around the corner of a house or around ill-fitting window frames makes odd sounds. The strange part was that the sound had seemed to come, not from a corner of the house or even from the wall in which my bedroom windows were set, but from some other part of the room. Well, I would mention it to Brian in the morning. Perhaps he knew the explanation.

Soon after I got back into bed the sound began again. But now, knowing what it was, I could ignore it. I fell asleep.

A knocking awoke me. In momentary confusion, I looked around the sun-flooded room and then called out, "Come in."

"No need for that." It was Mrs. Brill's voice. "I just wanted you to know that the family still has breakfast buffet style in the dining room."

I looked at my watch, which pointed to almost eight, and then got out of bed and dressed in jeans and a light blue pullover.

When I reached the dining room I found Brian helping himself to scrambled eggs and sausages from chafing dishes on the buffet. When we had exchanged good mornings I asked, "Eunice and Dale not down yet?"

"No. I guess they're tired from all that traveling yesterday."

That, and other things. I spooned eggs onto a plate and added a slice of toast.

When we had both sat down at the table, Brian asked, "Did you sleep well?"

"Not entirely. There was some sort of noise in my room last night."

"Noise!" The broad face beneath the brown hair showed mild surprise.

"Yes, a kind of crying, or whining. After a while I became sure it was the wind, even though the sound seemed to be coming from somewhere inside the room. Did Karen ever complain—"

54

I broke off, appalled. When I had descended to the lower floor a few minutes before there had been a youngish red-haired woman in a maid's uniform in the hall, polishing a mirror a few yards back beyond the foot of the steps. If she had remained there she was well out of earshot. Still, I might not be so lucky next time.

Apparently Brian had noticed my slip because his usually bland face looked worried. "You ought to try the sausages," he said. "They're good." Then, casually, "Like to take a little walk after breakfast?"

So that we could talk about the crying sound. "Love to," I said.

When Brian and I walked out the front door around a quarter of nine, his sister and Dale Carling still had not appeared. It was a sunny morning with a sky that the wind of the night before had polished to a bright blue. There was still a slight wind bending the tops of the tallest pines that bordered the curving drive, and stirring the blossom-laden branches of some ornamental fruit trees in the lawn's center.

As we walked along the graveled drive, Brian said, "I've thought of what might have caused that noise. Back in the eighteen-eighties Samuel Andexter—he was my grandfather—installed gas in the house for lighting and heating. A year or so later a heater leaked in one of the maid's rooms, and the girl almost died. Samuel got the notion of installing vents in all the family bedrooms—although not in the servants' rooms!—with outlets on the roof. I imagine whoever did the job must have told him that the vents would add to the heating cost without greatly lessening the danger, but Samuel had the work done anyway. When his son John, who later became Aunt Jo's husband, inherited the place, he had

55

caps put on the vent outlets on the roof, but maybe one of them has come off, letting wind down through the vent."

"Did Karen ever complain of such noises in that room?"

His tone was mildly chiding. "Sort of made a slip back there at breakfast, didn't you? No, she didn't, not that I know of. But it may be that the vent cap stayed in place until sometime during the last eight years.

"Anyway," he went on, "I'll go up on the roof today to see what I can find. And with your permission I'll look to see just where the vent opens into your room."

"I wish you would."

By now we had circled the big lawn to a point almost directly opposite those fan-shaped front steps. Brian said, "Shall we go back? As you can guess from the flab I'm carrying, I'm not much of a one for exercise."

"If you don't mind, I'd like to walk through the woods for a while."

"Why not? A few feet back there we passed the entrance to a path. It will lead you straight to a lake. The Andexter land extends only about a mile from the house in that direction, and so the lake is just beyond the property line."

We turned back. At the entrance to the path I said goodbye to him and struck off through the woods. Now I experienced much of what I had dreamed of the past week amid the sights and sounds and smells of New York. Springy earth, strewn with evergreen needles. Pine fragrance in the air. Harsh calls of bluejays and the more musical voices of birds I did not know. Off to the right, a natural clearing carpeted with those wild geraniums Eunice had pointed out to me along the roadside the day before. The wind had roughened. I could hear it sough through the treetops. But down here on the ground the air was still and hot.

A glimpse of blue ahead. I quickened my pace. Then I was out on a sloping beach. I was so delighted with it all—the lake ruffled into little whitecaps, the green wall of pines on the opposite shore, and under my feet the grate of small rounded stones—that at first I did not realize that there was anyone else there. Then from the corner of my eye I saw movement. I turned my head. A small outboard motorboat had been drawn up onto the beach. A jeans-clad man, naked from the waist up despite the brisk air, stood beside the boat, staring at me. Evidently he had been working on the boat's engine because, eyes still fixed on me, he was wiping his hands on a bit of waste. He dropped the piece of paper or cloth or whatever it was into the boat. Then he moved toward me, sneaker-clad feet almost noiseless over the clean white stones. There was a subtle menace about that advancing figure. I had an impulse to turn and run from him up to the path. But surely there was no need. this was the Maine woods, not Central Park.

And besides, I realized, with that odd fear still speeding my pulses, he was at least six feet to my five-feet-seven-inches. He would have no trouble overtaking me.

He stopped a few feet away. He was thirty, or maybe a little more or less. Probably less, judging from the taut musculature of his tanned chest and stomach. His face had almost harsh planes—high cheekbones, a nose that might have been broken sometime in the past, lips compressed into a straight line, a square chin. His brownish-blond hair, although curling at the neck, was cut short at the sides. His blue eyes had a cold blaze.

"So you came back. I'd never have thought you'd have the nerve."

He paused, and then added, "Amnesia victim! Do you expect anyone to believe that, Karen? Do you really?"

First Mrs. Brill and now this man. Both accepting me as Karen, both rejecting the story about my amnesia. What had she been like, that young girl, to make others jump to the immediate conclusion that she lied?

"Cat got your tongue? Oh, I see. I'm part of your amnesia, and you don't remember me. Well, the name is Joel Cartwright."

"Of course I remember you."

That cold blue gaze swept down to my shoes and then back up to my face. "You look as if you've grown an inch or so. Otherwise those eight years don't seem to have made much difference. Hard to believe, considering what you must have been up to all this time."

Up to? What on earth was he talking about?

I said, "Did you know I was coming back?"

He nodded. "When your cousin Eunice called from New York, your housekeeper told the delivery boy about it. Within an hour all of Muskeegan knew."

He paused and then went on, "When you first stepped out onto the beach, I saw you staring across at the boathouse."

"Boathouse?"

"Come off it, Karen!"

I turned and looked across the lake. I saw it then, a brown structure set in a small clearing above the beach. Beside it stood a white pickup truck which I presumed to be his. "Oh, yes. The boathouse."

"But it had just slipped your mind until now, huh—all those times we shacked up there. Although I never thought of it as shacking up," he said bitterly. "That would have been sacrilege! In spite of everything I was beginning to learn about you, to me you were beautiful, perfect, almost sacred—"

He broke off and then added with a harshness that mocked himself as well as me, "Tell me, do you still have that trick of digging your fingernails into a guy's shoulders to make him think he's really turned you on?"

I stared at him in dismay. So he was not only an enemy but an ex-lover. Why hadn't Eunice and Brian warned me about this Joel Cartwright? But then, at that time they must have been already in their forties. Probably the generation gap kept them from knowing about their teenage cousin's trysts in the boathouse with a slightly older lover.

I had to get away from there lest I make some irretrievable slip. I had to try to find out from Eunice or Brian as much as I could about this man—

"I suppose you didn't know that Danny's to be released in a few weeks," he said. "What's more, he'll be coming back here."

Who was Danny? And what was he to be released from? Hospital? Insane asylum? Jail?

"I'm sorry, but I'll have to say goodbye now, Joel."

"I thought the mention of Danny would shake you up!"

"I really have to get back. I promised my grandmother to—to read to her."

"Such solicitude. You put the old lady through hell for eight years, and then you come back and read Longfellow or somebody to her. Yes, you've certainly changed."

After a moment he added, frowning, "You really do

59

seem changed. Not just older and a little taller, but something else. The words you use, maybe—"

"I really must go. Goodbye."

I turned and hurried, feet grating over the white stones, toward the entrance to the path. He did not try to stop me.

CHAPTER **6**

THE HANDS of my watch pointed to a little past eleven when I emerged from the path onto the Pinehaven driveway. I hesitated, looking at the house. Somehow I did not want to go inside just then, or to talk to any of the Andexters. My conversation with Joel Cartwright had left me badly shaken. It did little good to remind myself that it was not I whom he hated. His hostility still had seemed almost like a physical force, lashing me.

Better to wait until I had quieted down. If Eunice and Brian knew how upset I had been by my first encounter with someone outside this house, they might decide that their whole idea had been a mistake and that it was best that Karen Andexter run away again. And I did not want to go back to New York. It was not just reluctance to forego the promised money that made me want to stay here. It was the thought of snatching happiness away from Karen's grandmother after she had enjoyed it for only a little while.

And so instead of entering the house I followed the drive around one corner to the rear. I found more lawn back there, set with a garden of rose trees not yet in bloom. On a pedestal in the rose garden's center a smiling stone cupid stood poised on one foot, aiming his bow. Beyond the rose garden stretched more lawn. Beyond that was a wide garage, a tennis court, a greenhouse, and another outbuilding. If I remembered Brian's sketch correctly, that building housed his studio. The garage's door was up, revealing a yellow sport car—a Porsche?—as well as the Bentley. Hazzard was polishing the stately old vehicle.

Beyond the outbuilding stretched more pinewood, sloping upward toward a distant, cone-shaped mountain.

I looked to my right. A flagstone path led to what must have been an addition to the house, since it had little relation to the formal facade. It was a glassed-in, semicircular porch jutting out onto the lawn. Beyond the glass I could see Eunice standing at an easel. She waved to me with her left hand, the one not holding a paintbrush. I waved and started to turn away. Then, hearing her tap on the glass, I turned back. She beckoned to me. Reluctant, still feeling upset by my encounter with Joel Cartwright, I moved toward her.

A door, also of glass, led onto the porch. I opened it and stepped into the warm air filled with the pleasant smell of ferns and other houseplants. They had been placed on metal stands flanking another door, a solid oak one set in the rear wall of the house. There were three armchairs of white wicker, and a circular glass coffee table.

"Good morning," Eunice said. "I was going to work outdoors, but it is too windy."

"Do you mind if I look at what you're painting?"

"In a moment. I want to finish this corner first. Just sit down. It won't bother me in the least if we talk." She threw a glance over her shoulder toward that solid-looking door and then added, "And it won't matter what we say as long as we keep our voices down."

I sat down in one of the armchairs. How dignified, even prim, she looked. It was hard to realize that only a few hours before she had been lying in Dale Carling's arms. She looked, frowning, through the glass, and then added a stroke to her canvas. I asked, "Are you painting the mountain?"

"Old Blue? No, the rose garden."

"That seems an odd name for a mountain."

"Not really. Often toward evening it looks almost cobalt blue."

"Is it part of a forest preserve?"

She smiled. "No, Aunt Jo owns it."

It seemed strange to me that any individual, particularly that fragile creature upstairs, should own a whole mountain.

"Are there ski trails up there?"

She threw me an oddly startled look. "No, but there should be. That mountain could offer even better skiing than Sugarloaf."

She worked in silence for a moment and then said, "The rose garden will be beautiful about ten days from now."

"Who does the gardening?"

"Hazzard is the official gardener as well as the chauffeur. But he really just supervises. Most of the actual work is done by a couple of teenage boys from Muskeegan."

Muskeegan. Joel Cartwright had mentioned that near-by town.

"I walked down to the lake this morning. A young man named Joel Cartwright was there . . ."

Eyes still fixed on her canvas, she said, "Oh, yes. Joel. His father owns one of the three garages in town."

"What else do you know about him?"

"Not much. He went away to college about ten years ago—Yale, I think it was. But a few months before he was to graduate, his father had a stroke, and Joel had to come home to run the family business."

"Was Karen still here then?"

"When Joel had to leave college?"

"Yes."

"Let me try to remember. No, I believe she had already run away by then."

And so it must have been during his summer vacations from college that he and Karen had "shacked up" in the boathouse. "Did you know that he and Karen had an affair?"

"No." Her tone held faint interest. "And he mentioned it today?"

"It would be more accurate to say that he threw it in my face."

She gave me an alarmed look. "You didn't—"

"No, I managed to keep my cool. I mean, I didn't give myself away." I paused and then asked, "Who is Danny?"

"Danny Cartwright? He's Joel's brother. A year or so younger, I think."

"Where is he now?"

"Why do you ask? Did Joel speak of him? I suppose he must have."

64

"He certainly did. And then he said, 'I thought the mention of Danny would shake you up.' "

She laid her brush in the long groove in the easel's lower edge. Turning to me, she said in a reluctant voice, "I'm sorry if it upsets you, but probably you would have had to hear about it sooner or later. Not long before Karen ran away, Danny Cartwright was stopped by the police on a Florida highway. They found a large amount of cocaine in his car. There was a scuffle and Danny hit one of the officers over the head with a tire iron. The man didn't die, but the Florida court gave Danny the maximum sentence on the combined charges. Drug dealing, I mean, and assault with a deadly weapon."

I said, after a moment, "But what did all that have to do with Karen?"

"I'm not sure. But there was talk that she had persuaded Danny to run the cocaine up from Florida. You see, he was young, perhaps not more than a few months older that Karen herself. And probably he as well as Joel was infatuated with her. Maybe he wanted to impress her with his daring. Maybe he hoped that if he made a lot of money he could cut his big brother out."

And now Danny was about to be released. No longer a teenager, but a prison-hardened man in his middle twenties. Did he carry a grudge against Karen Andexter? Or was it just his older brother who carried a grudge? I recalled the bitterness with which Joel had spoken of how he once felt about Karen. No doubt he hated her for her betrayal of him as much as for her supposed disastrous influence on his younger brother.

Should I tell Eunice that Danny Cartwright was to be released soon? No, I decided, at least not yet. There was no immediate danger. But if Eunice and her brother knew that in a short time a perhaps revenge-bent ex-convict was to appear upon the scene, they might decide that it would be best to send me back to where I came from.

Eunice had resumed her painting. She made a few strokes and then said, "Would you like to look now?"

I rose and stood beside her.

In the background, a hazy suggestion of cone-shaped Old Blue rising out of the pine forest. In the foreground, the smooth lawn and the rose garden with its bloomless but leafed-out rose trees and its naked cupid.

But what had she done to the cupid?

I had a sudden memory of a coffee table book I had looked through when I shared an apartment with those other two would-be actresses. A Christmas gift to one of my roommates, the book had consisted of reproductions of modern paintings hung in the Jeu de Paume Museum in Paris. Among them had been one of Van Gogh's early works, a portrait of two little girls. Even though it had been painted years before he had sent his severed ear to a prostitute he had fallen in love with, you could see his incipient madness on the canvas. It was in the subtle distortion of the little girls' faces, a twisting of the features so that they expressed a most unchildlike blend of anger and anxiety.

Something similar had happened to the cupid's bland stone face. On Eunice Andexter's canvas his smile had become a leer. Beneath the curly locks there seemed to be bumps suggestive of budding horns.

Again I thought of how Dale Carling had said there was a strain of "eccentricity" in the Andexters.

Someone knocked briefly on the other side of the door leading into the house, thus saving me from the necessity

66

of making some comment about her work. As Eunice and I turned around, her brother opened the door and stepped out onto the glassed-in porch.

He said, "I've been looking for you, Karen, for a couple of reasons. First, I went up onto the roof a little while ago. I was right. One of those vent caps had come off. I've put it back in place. And so from now on you shouldn't hear any odd noises in the night."

Evidently he had already told his sister about the sounds because she asked no questions. "Thank you," I said.

"As for the vent's outlet in your bedroom, it's covered with a grill. You'll find it between your dressing table and the wardrobe."

Again I thanked him and then asked, "And the other reason you were looking for me?"

"I have a message from your grandmother. She'd like you to have lunch with her in her sitting room."

"I'll go up there right away." As I walked through the doorway into the house, I suddenly wondered about Brian's sculpture. If I saw it, would I find in it the same disquieting element I saw in his sister's work?

In most ways I thoroughly enjoyed that luncheon with Josephine Andexter. I enjoyed the food, broiled sole and buttered carrots and a green salad. I liked sitting with her at the small table drawn close to a window overlooking the front lawn.

But one thing I found painful. More than once she said, "Darling, do you remember—" and then broke off, cheeks flushing.

Finally I said, "Please! Talk about the past if you want to."

"But Karen! That psychiatrist in New York! He told

67

Eunice and Brian that you must never be badgered with questions about what you do or don't remember."

"You're not badgering me. Talk about whatever you like. If I find it is making me nervous I'll let you know."

She said hesitantly, "Well, I was just about to say something about that pony you had when you were five. You named him Doolie, for some reason no one could understand, and you cried terribly when he got glanders and had to be put down."

I gave her a noncommittal smile and a nod.

Throughout the rest of the meal she talked happily about the pony, and about "looking out this very window to see you giving doll tea parties on the lawn," and of "the time I took you into Muskeegan to see that Disney movie."

The red-haired maid Edith finally came in to take our plates away. When the maid had gone, Mrs. Andexter said tentatively, "Karen."

"Yes?"

She nodded toward the two long bookcases, each about four feet high, on the opposite side of the room. "Would you mind reading to me for a while?"

"I'd love to. What would you like to hear?" I wondered what she would choose. Dickens? Jane Austen? Or, as Joel Cartwright had suggested sardonically, Longfellow?

"I'd like *The Great Gatsby*."

I almost gave a startled laugh. And then I realized that there was nothing strange in her choice. Fitzgerald had been a contemporary of hers. Somehow, though, despite that old shipboard photograph of her in a cloche hat and loose, knee-length frock, until now I had not thought of her as a member of the Jazz Age generation.

As I walked toward the bookshelves she said, "The

68

books are arranged alphabetically by author. Look under F.—F. Scott Fitzgerald wrote it."

Karen, I reflected, could not have been a bookish type if her grandmother felt she had to tell her who wrote *Gatsby*. "Here it is," I said.

For more than an hour we were both absorbed by the East Egg bootlegger, and his parties, and his friend who fixed the World Series, and his stubborn love for frivolous Daisy. Then Mrs. Andexter said, "Your voice is beginning to sound tired, child. And you look a little tired, too. Why don't you take a nap?"

"Perhaps I shall. I didn't sleep too well last night." I paused. "Shall I come back here and have dinner with you?'

"No, darling. I eat very little in the evening, and I go to bed very early. But if you could join me for lunch whenever possible from now on—"

"I'd love to." I replaced the book and then came back across the room to kiss her cheek. "Until tomorrow, Grandmother."

With a slight sense of shock I realized that it felt very natural to call her Grandmother.

I must have been more tired than I had realized. Near sunset light was filling my bedroom when I awoke from my nap. I took a quick shower to help myself wake up. I had just finished dressing in a yellow cotton shift when I heard the soft sound of the dinner gong.

The atmosphere in the dining room that night was strained. Without Josephine Andexter's presence to remind us that we were all playing a part, we had to be doubly guarded in our speech lest Mrs. Brill walk in at just the wrong moment. I said almost nothing. Eunice chatted with the men on such safe subjects as the freak storms striking the West Coast and a Washington scandal involving a senator and a woman cabinet member.

We were eating a dessert of lemon ice when Dale Carling said, "Karen, would you like to go into town for a bit of local nightlife? We could go to Marty's. As you probably remember, that's the most popular spot."

"You mean, all four of us?"

"Don't include me," Brian said. "I want to work."

Eunice said, "I'd also rather stay home. There's something on Channel Eight that I don't want to miss."

"Looks as if it will have to be just the two of us," Dale said.

"Yes, Karen," Eunice said. "Why don't you two just run along? Marty's is no more formal than it used to be. That dress you have on will do just fine."

There was no trace of pique in her voice. Instead she sounded pleasantly matter-of-fact. Even though Dale so far had shown no sign of finding me attractive, it still seemed strange that she should urge her lover to spend the evening with a woman only about half her own age.

I had a sudden uneasy feeling that when it came to sophistication, I, the Manhattan career girl, was not in the same league with these middle-aged downeasters and their Connecticut friend.

"All right," I said.

CHAPTER 7

HALF AN HOUR LATER I sat beside Dale in the yellow Porsche. The rushing beam of its headlights cast a refracted glow on the tall pines walling both sides of the road.

I said, "Correct me if I'm wrong, but I have a feeling that the purpose of this excursion is something more than amusement."

"So it is. If there's even a chance that a suspicion might arise in Muskeegan that you are not Karen, we want to nip it in the bud. The best way to do that is to make it clear that the Andexter household has accepted you completely."

"And so you, as a member of that household, will appear with me publicly in one of the local nightspots."

"Exactly."

"But what if we are approached by someone Karen Andexter would be expected to know?"

"If that should happen, and it probably will, I think you're bright enough to follow my lead. And what if you do display a bit of confusion and uncertainty? Would that be so surprising in an amnesiac?"

"I suppose you're right."

For a while after that there was no sound except the car's smooth hum. Once some sort of night bird—a hawk, perhaps—flew across the headlights' path, wings beating soundlessly. Then we began to pass a few houses standing with lighted windows beyond the first line of trees. The dirt road became a paved one. Soon there were no more woods, just houses, and then abruptly we were driving through Muskeegan's business district.

At a little past nine, the town was wide awake. Apparently the movie theater's first show had just ended. People were streaming across the outer lobby, past the short line of ticket-buyers at the box office. ("They're the smart young in-crowd," Dale said, smiling. "They never go to the early show.") Pedestrians moved leisurely along the sidewalks or stood looking at window displays of furniture or clothing or hardware.

Marty's Tavern, with a big green neon sign above its double doors, stood on the far edge of town. We left the Porsche in the parking lot and walked toward the entrance. I became aware that my nerves had tightened. Would the people beyond those swinging doors believe, as Mrs. Brill and Joel Cartwright had believed, that I was Karen Andexter? Probably they would. But I hoped that no one in the place would look at me as the housekeeper and the young garage operator had. To read such hostility in another's face is unpleasant enough even when you know the reason for it. When you don't, you feel both bewildered and frightened.

We went in. To our right were at least fifteen tables covered with blue-and-white-checked tablecloths. About

72

half the tables were occupied by couples or groups. To our left was a long bar, with several customers perched on high stools.

Behind the bar, drying a glass beer mug, stood a stocky man of forty-odd. Dark hair carefully combed over his head had separated into strands, revealing a bald pate.

"Evening, Carl." Dale spoke through the sound of a Dolly Parton number issuing from a loudspeaker above the bar mirror. "Karen, this is Carl Sims. Karen Andexter, Carl. You two wouldn't have known each other," he said, turning to me. "Carl came here from Augusta six years ago and bought Marty's."

"How'd do, Miss Andexter." Even though he might not have known Karen, he had certainly heard of her return. The curiosity in his dark eyes told me that. But when he spoke it was in reply to Dale's comment. "Best move I ever made, coming here from Augusta." He looked complacently around the room. "Damned good crowd for a week night, I'd say. You folks going to sit at the bar?"

Dale looked at me. "You'd rather sit at a table, wouldn't you?"

I nodded.

"Okay," Marty said, "I'll send someone to take your order."

As we threaded our way between the tables toward a vacant one, I was aware of curious stares. Twice I heard Dale say, "Hello, there!" but both times, hand on my elbow, he kept me moving. Finally we sat down at a table at least a dozen feet from the nearest occupied one. With my back to the other customers, I could look across a small dance floor, empty at the moment, to an arched doorway. Above it, shadow-box signs of etched glass, one showing a man's profile, the other a woman's, indicated

73

that somewhere beyond were the restrooms. At right angles to the arch was a door marked "Exit," evidently leading to the parking lot.

A freckled young woman with sandy hair took our order, a scotch-and-water for Dale and a glass of beer for me. After she had brought our drinks, we talked for a few moments about the music now issuing from the loudspeaker. It was a song by Ronald Reagan's favorite vocalist, Merle Haggard.

Then I said, "You spoke to people a few minutes ago, but you didn't introduce me."

He shrugged. "Why push our luck? They saw me introduce you to Carl, and that should be enough. Of course, if someone comes over to our table—"

He broke off. The appalled look on his face told me that someone was coming toward our table at that very moment, someone he did not want to see.

Then, smiling, he got to his feet. "Why, hello, Betty. How nice to see you."

"Is it?"

She was a plump, blondish woman in dark pants of some synthetic material and a light blue blouse hanging loose over her waistline. Glasses with pink rims in a shape that suggested butterfly wings gave her a skittish look. I judged her to be in her midforties. And I could tell that she was quite drunk.

"Betty, this is Karen Andexter. Betty Gadsen, Karen." He added, "Join us, won't you?"

Instead of answering, she lowered herself into a chair and sat looking at me from slightly bloodshot and distinctly hostile hazel eyes. Dale said, "Of course, it may be that you two used to know each other." I felt that I could detect a certain nervousness in his smooth voice.

74

I said cautiously, "Yes, I think I do—"

"Don't try to be polite," she snapped. "I mean, you don't have to pretend you remember me. The only time you and I saw anything of each other was when you were fifteen. I was scrub nurse the day you had your tonsils out."

"Betty is now one of the assistant head nurses at Muskeegan Hospital." Dale's admiring tone, I felt, was meant to placate her.

Not answering him, she continued to look at me. "You look older, of course." Then, turning to Dale: "But I'm still surprised to see her with you. You've always let me think that the under-thirties left you cold."

"Betty, Betty! It's not like that. The Andexters feel that after all this time Karen should be reintroduced to her hometown, so to speak. As a friend of the family, I asked her if she'd like to come here tonight."

When she didn't answer, but just looked at him with brooding eyes, he added, "Don't you believe me?"

Instead of replying, she countered, "Have you and I still got a date for Friday night?"

"Of course. Dinner at the hotel. I'll pick you up at seven."

"You'd better." Her tone, like her gaze, was brooding.

"Now, Betty. Don't act like this. Tell me what you want to drink."

A bit unsteadily, she got to her feet. "No, thanks. I came in here for a drink, but now I think I'll just go home."

He too had stood up. "Perhaps that would be a good idea."

She said, with a swift belligerence that must have made him regret his words, "Are you trying to say that

75

I'm getting to be a lush?"

"Of course not! It's just that you look a little tired and—"

"Lush or not, I've still got enough brains to know when I've got *you* over a barrel. See you Friday night," she added, and started an unsteady course between the tables toward the door.

For perhaps a minute Dale and I sat in silence. Strange, I thought. I could understand his affair with Eunice Andexter. She was attractive enough in a middle-aged, country-gentlewoman sort of way. But this woman!

Dale must have signaled the waitress because she set two more drinks on the table. When she had gone I said, "That nurse. She seemed so—hostile."

"Not really. I mean, Betty Gadsen doesn't turn hostile unless she's drinking."

"But that last remark of hers, something about having you over a barrel—"

"I have no idea what she meant by that." Then, with a smile that almost but not quite took the sting out of his words: "Anyway, it's scarcely any of your business, is it?"

He was quite right. His love life, no matter how strange or complicated, was none of my business. I started to sip my beer and then sat frozen, with the glass mug poised in midair.

Back turned to me, Joel Cartwright now sat at the bar. He was looking at my reflection in the mirror, his face still and cold above the open neck of a brown sport shirt.

I felt color warm my cheeks, almost as if I merited the scornful accusation in his eyes. Then anger surged through me. Suppose that I really had been Karen. Suppose that, at eighteen, I had behaved frivolously or

76

promiscuously or even unlawfully. Even so, was his attitude justified? What sort of man could carry a grudge against a teenager all these years?

I felt a sudden urge to get out of this place. I turned to Dale. "Do you mind if we—"

"Well, well! What have we here?"

Startled, I looked up at the short, smiling man who stood with his hands on the back of the chair Betty Gadsen had vacated. He was fifty or a little more and wore khaki pants and shirt, with his stomach bulging over his belt. His head was bald except for a fringe of graying brown hair. Despite his friendly smile, his small, light blue eyes had a slyly triumphant look, a look that seemed to say that everyone had something disreputable to hide and that he was a man who sooner or later would ferret it out.

Dale said, "Why, hello, Chief. Karen, this is George Tate, our chief of police."

"No need for introductions," the chief said. "You being sort of new around here might not know it, but Karen and I are old friends. Mind if I join you?"

Even before Dale was able to say "Why, of course not," the other man had pulled out the chair. He sat down.

"You do remember me, don't you, Karen?"

I said nervously, "Why, of course."

"I thought you would. When I heard you were coming back, I said to myself, 'She'll remember old George, even if she can't remember why she left Muskeegan, or what happened after that.' "

Those little blue eyes, scanning my face, seemed to be saying that he could imagine what had been happening to me during the last eight years. I had an irrational sense of being soiled, almost as if I were guilty of the things his expression implied.

I said, "Will you excuse us? We were just about to leave."

Dale must have been aware of my distress, because he said, "Yes, it's getting late."

"No, you don't!" One of his plump hands pushed down on Dale's shoulder. He added, with jovial menace, "You want me to arrest you for resisting an officer?" He turned and said to the sandy-haired girl who was hurrying past with a tray of beer mugs, "Bring me a rye-and-water. And refills for these folks."

Lifting my barely touched glass mug, I said, "We don't need refills."

He said, still with that playfully threatening air, "You'll take it and like it." Then, after a pause: "You notice there's an old boyfriend of yours at the bar?"

Unable to think of a reply, I said nothing.

He persisted, "You hear that jailbird brother of his is getting paroled?"

Involuntarily I looked toward the bar. Joel Cartwright's gaze, coldly watchful, was still fixed on our table. Suddenly I felt I could not stay another moment under the gaze of those two men, Joel's accusatory, and the fat man's cynical and derisive.

The waitress was placing glasses on the table. I said, standing up, "Excuse me, please." I hurried past the still-empty dance floor, under the arch, and down the corridor to the ladies' room.

In the mirror above the wash basin my face looked flushed. I patted my cheeks with a moistened paper towel and ran cold water over my wrists. I renewed my lipstick. Then I sat down in the room's sole chair, a straight wooden one. Maybe if I stayed in here long enough I would find that loathsome police chief gone when I came out.

But soon the door opened and three girls entered. Perhaps they had not known Karen, for none of them spoke to me. But I could tell from their avid side glances that they had heard things about her. I got up, opened the door, and walked down the dim corridor.

When I reached the archway I stopped and looked out into the main room. George Tate still sat talking to Dale. On impulse I turned and went out the exit door into the parking lot.

The darkness, broken only by the amber glow of a few spotlights under the tavern's eaves, was soothing after the noise and glare inside. I found the Porsche and leaned against its side. Here there were only faint sounds, the muted strains of a Willie Nelson record inside the building and the occasional hum of a car along the street. For the first time since I had broken the smoking habit five years earlier, I found myself wanting a cigarette.

Footsteps over the parking lot gravel. A burly shape moving toward me. "Thought you'd get away, didn't you? I saw you duck out here." I realized then that he was at least a little drunk. "Is that any way to treat old George?"

Plump hands grasped my shoulders and pressed me back against the side of the car. I tried to twist away. Hands tightening their grip he said, "Now look here, you little bitch," which gave me a hysterical desire to laugh because I had just become aware that our faces were on a level.

But he was a lot stronger than I was. Now that fat stomach was pressing against me. I said, "Do you want me to scream? Do you?"

"Go ahead. Wouldn't be the first time somebody I was arresting kicked up a fuss."

"Arresting! What on earth—"

"Sure. Marijuana possession. Four ounces. I got the evidence right here in my pocket. How would your grandmother feel about that, on top of everything else you've put her through? Back only a day or two and already you're in trouble."

I said slowly, "Why, you unspeakable—"

One of his hands left my shoulder and grasped my face, fingers biting into my cheeks. "None of that now!" he said playfully. And then, not at all playfully: "But I really did catch you with some stuff once, didn't I? You and Danny Cartwright and a couple of other kids were having a little reefer party in the woods—"

I tried to wrench my face free of those imprisoning fingers. "Let go of me!"

"It was not long after you'd been kicked out of that fancy school in Connecticut, and you were anxious not to get into more trouble. So you let me know what you'd do for me if I decided not to run you in. But you didn't pay off, did you? Always promising to meet me on one of the backroads and then never showing up. And then in the fall you just disappeared.

"Well, you're back here now, and you're not going to make a fool of me again, not this time—"

His lips, rubbery and moist, came down on mine. I fought him, trying to get one hand free to claw at his face, trying and failing to kick his shins.

Then suddenly I was free and George Tate was staggering back against the side of a parked pickup truck. A foot or so to my left, Joel Cartwright loomed tall in the semidarkness.

80

"Better go home and sleep it off, Chief."

Perhaps the fat man had been a little drunk only minutes before, but now he sounded cold sober—and vicious. "Who the hell do you think you are, Cartwright?" He had straightened up and was rubbing one shoulder. It must have banged against the truck's sideview mirror. "I'll tell you who you are. You're a small-town garageman. You want to get a flock of summonses? I can always find something, you know. A sign closer to the sidewalk than the law says, or—"

"You don't scare me." Joel's voice was cold. "Maybe you still scare some people, but not me."

"Aahh!" Dignified disgust in the older man's tone. "What's the point in talking to you?"

He walked away through the sparsely filled parking lot. Joel and I turned to watch him. Evidently his car, if he had come in one, was parked on the street because he disappeared around the tavern's front corner.

I said into the silence, "How did you know—"

"I saw him follow you out here. And I know George."

He probably also knew, I reflected, about the man's frustrated pursuit of Karen Andexter eight years before.

"Will he really make trouble for you?"

"Oh, I don't think so. Once he could throw his weight around. But people are getting sick of it. He barely squeaked through the last election, and he may get thrown out in the next one if he doesn't watch his step."

He opened the Porsche's door. "Get in. I'll tell Carling you're out here." He closed the door and without another word walked away.

Perhaps two minutes passed. Then I saw Dale Carling come out the tavern's side door. He got into the driver's seat. "I didn't know you were out here. I thought you were still back in the ladies' room hoping Tate would leave. In fact, I was about to send the waitress back to tell you he'd left the place."

Dale started the car, drove out of the lot. When we had turned onto the main street he said, "What happened back there?"

I told him.

Dale said, "Sorry about that. But as I said, I had no idea you were out there. When the chief went out the side door I figured he was just going to get into his car and drive away."

"Well, no real harm done." After a moment I asked, "Why was Karen expelled from that private school?"

"I'm not sure. I was still in Bangor then, you know."

"Could it have had anything to do with marijuana?"

"Come to think of it, I recall Eunice and Brian saying that it did. Karen and a couple of other girls were caught smoking grass in the dormitory."

For a long while we drove in silence. More and more I was feeling haunted by her, that girl who, at least when we were both teenagers, had looked so very much like me. That girl who bedded down with Joel, and at least flirted with his younger brother, and led that police chief on a long chase. That contradictory girl who had written a loving "poem" to her grandmother and then broken the woman's heart by disappearing. As the car followed the yellow beam of its headlights along the forest-walled road, I had an eerie feeling that if I turned my head I would see Karen, or the ghost of her, running along inside the first line of trees.

We had almost reached the house when I said, "I've been meaning to ask. Is this your car?"

"No, I left mine in Bangor. This car is for any member

of the household who wants to use it. I'm sure there would be no objection if you wanted to drive it into Muskeegan for shopping or whatnot."

"That's nice. Except," I said wryly, "that I don't relish much the idea of hanging out in Muskeegan, not after tonight."

"I can understand that. And I'm sorry that clown of a police chief gave you a bad time. But at least we can be fairly certain now that no one is going to doubt that you're Karen."

He let me off at the foot of the steps and then drove around the corner of the house toward the garage. I climbed to the unlocked front door and went into the hall. Apparently either Brian or Eunice was still up. I could see light spilling from the library doorway into the semidarkened hall.

I looked at my watch. Ten-twenty. Surely it was later than that. I held the watch to my ear and verified that it had stopped. The grandfather clock stood beside a wall table a few feet beyond the foot of the stairs. I walked to it and saw that the big hands pointed to almost twelve-thirty. I set my watch, wound it, and then climbed the stairs to my room.

Minutes later, in my nightgown, I sat at the dressing table brushing my hair. Suddenly I became aware that I had not set my handbag down among all those framed photographs on its glass surface. I turned on the bench and threw a glance around the room. No handbag visible. But surely I'd had it with me when I entered the house.

Then I remembered. I had set the bag down on the wall table while I adjusted my watch. It must be there still.

Better to get it. Not that it contained anything of value, or anything that could identify me to the servants as someone other than Karen Andexter. Items I'd always carried with me in New Your—bankbook, department store chargeplates, driver's license, Social Security card—were all stowed away in my locked suitcase. Still, it didn't look good to have a personal belonging of mine cluttering up the downstairs. I put on a robe, went out into the hall, and walked to the landing.

Dale Carling and Brian Andexter stood down there facing each other. Dale had placed his hands on the other man's shoulders. A little taller than his companion, he was smiling down into Brian's face.

I turned away and moved back toward my room. Never mind my handbag. I'd get it in the morning.

I don't think I'm a prude. As someone on at least the fringes of show business, I knew homosexuals and counted some of them as my friends. But somehow the thought of Dale Carling and Eunice and her brother carrying on a *ménage à trois* in this isolated old house upset me.

But it was none of my business, not in the least. I went into my room and closed the door.

CHAPTER 8

A LITTLE AFTER EIGHT the next morning I awoke to gray stillness. When I went to the window I saw high, scudding clouds, but apparently no wind disturbed the lower atmosphere because on the far side of the lawn the pine trees stood motionless.

No wind. Was that why no sounds in the night had disturbed my sleep? Or was it because Brian, by recapping the vent's outlet on the roof, had shut out the air currents that had moved along it, whispering and crying, my first night in this house?

The vent. Its outlet in this room, Brian had said, was between the dressing table and the wardrobe. Yesterday, distracted by other matters, I had not looked for it myself, but now, still in my nightgown, I turned from the window and walked across the room. Yes, there it was, a dark metal grill of about a foot square set fifteen inches or so above the white baseboard.

When I went down to the dining room I found it

empty. However, there were only two pieces of toast left in the rack and two small sausages and a few tablespoons of scrambled eggs in the chafing dishes, and so I knew that Brian and Dale and perhaps Eunice had breakfasted earlier. I heaped the remaining food on my plate, poured a cup of coffee, and sat down.

What should I do until it was time to join Josephine Andexter for lunch? Well, perhaps I should walk down to that pretty lake again. The day before, because of Joel Cartwright's distracting presence, I had not been able to enjoy it fully.

It was not until I left the dining room that I remembered my handbag. There it was, still on the hall table where I had left it the night before. I took it up to my room, set it on the dressing table, and put on my white sweater.

Walking along the path through the woods a few minutes later, I realized that I needn't have worn the sweater. Here beneath the trees the air was close. As if oppressed by the overcast stillness, the birds were quieter than the day before, and the few squirrels I saw, less frisky and voluble.

A glimpse of glass-smooth blue water ahead. I emerged from the woods into cooler air. A few feet to my left, Joel Cartwright sat beside the boat he had pulled up onto the rocky beach. My pulses quickened. I had to realize then what I had not acknowledged to myself earlier. I had hoped he would be here.

He stood up and walked toward me, his expression only a little less cold than it had been as he watched me in the bar mirror the night before. He said, without preamble, "You okay?"

"Why—why, yes."

"I thought maybe George Tate had roughed you up a little."

"Not really." I paused and then added, "You walked off last night before I got a chance to thank you."

"That's all right."

We looked unsmilingly at each other through the gray light. I knew that now I should say good morning and then turn and walk away along the beach. I should do it for all sorts of reasons.

But I didn't. I opened my mouth to say, "Do you come here a lot?" and then realized I had better amend that. I asked, "Do you still come here a lot?"

He nodded. "Several mornings a week when the weather's good. You see, from noon until eight o'clock closing I'm at the garage."

"It must be nice to start the day like that, floating around on the lake."

The look he gave me told me that I must have blundered. "I don't just float. I still take fishing tackle with me."

"Oh, of course."

"And when the striped bass are running I still go over to Wrecker's Point."

Something about the way he spoke told me that Wrecker's Point was associated in his mind with more than striped bass. He went on, "I don't suppose you've been over to the point yet since you—came back."

"Not yet."

The silence lengthened. He continued to look at me with aloof blue eyes. What was he thinking behind that poker face? About how much, or how little, I had changed in appearance? Was he wondering how I had spent the past eight years? Or was he thinking about how his younger brother had spent them, shut away in a Florida prison?

On sudden impulse I asked, "Do you see your brother often?"

"I get down there as often as I can."

The increased coldness of his tone made me wish I had not brought the subject up. But now that I had, I might as well try to learn as much as I could. If I went on as I had been, flying almost entirely blind, I might make errors I could not mend.

"And Danny is coming back here when he is released?"

"Of course. He'll work in the garage. It isn't easy for an ex-con to get a job, you know."

His voice had become downright harsh. Nevertheless, I persisted. "What does he think of me now?"

"I don't know. I don't think he's even mentioned you to me in the last five or six years. And even before that he was a hell of a lot more forgiving than I was."

He paused. When I said nothing, he went on, "Even at the first, the kid didn't seem to really blame you for leading him into it."

For a moment I felt a surge of anger, almost as if it were in fact my younger self we were discussing. "After all, I was only eighteen!"

"Sure, just like Danny. But you were years older than him in sophistication. And that went double for those friends of yours."

"What friends?" I realized he would expect me to know the answer to that. But if need be I was prepared to say that my memory of the months before my disappearance was blurred.

Apparently, though, he was too angry to wonder at my question. "You know damned well what friends! Those girls who were kicked out of that school at the same time you were. And the older brother of one of them, that guy who took to running drugs up from Florida because he wasn't making enough money in his old man's brokerage firm."

He paused, as if waiting for me to speak, and then rushed on, "You thought the guy was great, didn't you? Real cool, as we used to say. You let Danny know that. And the poor stupid kid decided to get in touch with that amateur drug runner and see if he could get in on the business. He figured he'd be a big man in your eyes, big enough to cut me out and everyone else. Instead he ended up with twelve years in prison, and not even the chance of parole until he'd served six."

"I'm sorry," I said into the lengthening silence. "What else can I say beyond that?"

"Nothing, I suppose."

Not for the first time, I wondered how much of that hostility in his eyes was on his brother's behalf and how much provoked by the memory of his own jealous suffering. Whatever the answer, I had a sense that he was feeling something besides antagonism at the moment.

He said abruptly, "Well, so long for now. If I'm to catch any fish—"

"So long."

He turned toward his boat. I walked in the opposite direction over the smooth white stones. After a while I heard the outboard motor start. By the time I turned back toward the path's entrance he was out in the middle of the lake, threading bait onto a hook.

I turned onto the path. As I moved through the quiet woods I was uneasily aware that this third meeting with Joel Cartwright had disturbed me more, and in a different way, than yesterday's two encounters.

From now on I would stay away from the lake.

My afternoon with Josephine Andexter passed pleasantly. After lunch we settled down with *Gatsby*. After about an hour she said, "You're beginning to sound tired, dear. Better put the book away."

When I came back from the bookcase to sit beside her, I asked, "Did you ever happen to meet Fitzgerald?"

She looked startled. "No, but I saw him once, outside the Plaza Hotel in New York City."

"Would you tell me about it?"

She said, after a moment, "Are you sure you want me to?"

"Why, of course! What makes you think I wouldn't?"

"Because you used to find my stories boring. Oh, don't shake your head, my darling. I could tell you were bored."

"Well, I won't be bored now."

She told me then of how she and her husband, on a theater-and-shopping trip to New York, had emerged from the Plaza one evening to see a small crowd gathered around the courtyard fountain. "Fitzgerald and his wife Zelda were in the fountain basin, splashing water on each other. They were in evening clothes."

As I asked questions—Were they both drunk? What year was that? Did anyone call the police?—her cheeks turned pink with pleasure. Finally she patted my hand. "It's nice that you've changed in some ways, my darling. I used to feel—oh, a little wistful because you didn't want to hear what the world was like when I was young."

"I'm older myself now. Maybe that's why I'm more interested in the past."

A ray of sunlight came through the window and

touched her white curls. I looked out through the glass. Patches of blue were showing in the gray sky. "Grandmother, would you like me to take you for a drive sometime? I'll ask Emma and Brian if I may use the Porsche."

"Of course you may. It's really my car, you know, although Brian picked it out. You see, I still have not been able to persuade them to take any compensation for all they do for me. They wouldn't even take title to the Porsche. But at least I've been able to provide them with the use of it. And of course they like it better than the second car we used to have, that old Lincoln. I'm sure you remember the Lincoln."

Something must have flickered in my eyes because she said, in an appalled tone. "Oh, I'm sorry. I keep forgetting that I'm not supposed to ask you about what you do or don't remember."

"It's all *right*. I told you yesterday that it was. Now how about our taking a drive?"

"Darling, I find it too hard to get in and out of an automobile. But, please! Drive the Porsche whenever you like."

I almost said, "Last night Dale Carling and I drove into town in it." But of course I couldn't distress her with an account of that evening. And so all I said was "Thank you."

After a moment I added, "I understand that Dale Carling has been staying here only a few months. What do you think of him?"

"He seems like a very nice young man. He's certainly been charming to me. And Eunice and Brian say that he has been most helpful to them in managing my affairs." Then, swiftly: "Why, darling? Is there something about

91

him you don't like?' "

Naked fear in her face now. Fear that her beloved grandchild might find some reason—any reason—to disappear again.

"Oh, no! He's always been very pleasant to me." Which was true.

"And Eunice and Brian? Do you think you'll get along with them all right? As far as I know you did so in the past, but perhaps now—"

"Of course I'll get along with them. There's no reason why I shouldn't, especially since they are helpful to you." I paused and then said, momentarily off guard, "They're both quite attractive. I wonder why neither of them ever married."

"Why, it's because of poor Benjamin Andexter, of course."

After a moment I remembered. Dale Carling had told me that Benjamin, brother of Josephine's husband John, had been the father of Eunice and Brian. Afraid of saying the wrong thing, I said nothing at all.

"It must be a terrible thing to grow up knowing your father died mad. Although I must say that Eunice and Brian have always seemed to me as sane as anybody."

So Eunice and Brian's father had been insane. Well, except for that oddly distorted cupid in Eunice's painting, they had seemed entirely stable to me also. And even the painting was really no sort of evidence, I realized now. When Picasso first began painting his women with two noses, some people must have thought he had lost his mind.

I said, "I haven't seen any of Brian's work since—since I've been back. What is it like now?"

"His work? Oh, you mean his sculpture. Well, it's still

92

what they call abstract, which means I don't understand it. But some people must. He sells a piece every now and then."

Someone knocked. "That must be Dr. Brawley. Will you please let him in, Karen?" She added swiftly, "He knows you've come home."

Dr. Brawley, a pleasant-faced, wispy little man, looked to be almost as old as his patient. He said, "Well, well, Karen! Welcome home!" I could see all sorts of questions in the faded blue eyes behind the rimless glasses. But undoubtedly he also had heard that a New York psychiatrist had warned against "probing." Or perhaps it was concern for his patient, or just ordinary politeness. Anyway, he asked no questions. I shook his thin, dry hand, kissed Josephine Andexter's cheek, and left the room.

I went downstairs. A high-pitched whining sound came from the living room. I walked through its opened doors. Edith was dusting a mirror. Mrs. Brill, on a low stepstool, was running a hand vacuum over the window draperies that matched the gold brocade covering the stiffly formal sofas and chairs. At sight of me she shut off the vacuum and stepped down onto the floral rug.

I said, "Oh, I'm sorry. I didn't want to interrupt your work."

"Something you want?"

Despite the curtness of her words, her expression was less hostile than it had been when I first entered this house. I'd tried to make her more friendly. I had greeted her politely whenever we met in the halls, and smiled at her when she served me at dinner. Apparently Karen had behaved differently. I saw puzzlement in Mrs. Brill's eyes, combined with a grudging acknowledgment that perhaps I was somewhat more to her taste than I used to be.

"Do you happen to know where Mr. Carling is, or Mr. Andexter?"

"As far as I know, Mr. Carling's in his room. Mr. Andexter is out in his studio."

Thank heaven for that sketch Brian had drawn for me. Otherwise I might have found myself asking where his studio was. "Thank you, Mrs. Brill."

I went back along the hall, past the open door of the kitchen where the cook, a tall, dignified-looking blond woman, stood at a table rolling out dough on a slab of marble. I said hello, received a nod in return, and went out the rear door. The sun was out, I saw. A brisk breeze was hurrying the last of the clouds toward the southeast.

To my left was the glassed-in porch where Eunice had stood painting the day before. It was empty. I walked past it to the drive and then moved toward the garage. Its door was closed. In the glass-sided greenhouse next to the garage I could see Hazzard moving about among the benches crowded with potted plants and flats of seedlings. The small building next to it, I saw now, was probably some sort of tool shed, its wide door padlocked. But through the open door of the larger structure next to the shed came the sound of hammering. I walked to the doorway and stood looking in.

Light flooded through a skylight onto wide shelves bearing pieces of sculpture I vaguely thought of as "modern." Brian Andexter, in blue denim pants and shirt, stood at a work table hammering nails into what looked like a long box.

"Brian?"

He looked up. With a pleased smile spreading over his

94

face, he laid down his hammer. "Come in, come in. I've been wanting to show you my work."

I walked over the the table. "What's that you're building?"

"A form. You see, I work in cement. I'll fill this form with cement, let it dry, and then knock the wooden sides and bottom away."

He showed me the various sculptures on the shelves. Perhaps some or all of them were quite good. On the other hand, perhaps people who knew about such matters might have found them hopeless clichés. I did not feel competent to judge. There were spheres attached to columns. There was a rectangular slab of cement with holes of various sizes, suggesting—to me, at least—a slab of Swiss cheese. I murmured "Interesting," and "My!" and "How unusual," hoping he would find my comments adequate. He seemed to.

At last I said, "I came out here to ask you about the Porsche. Would it be all right if I drove it tomorrow?"

"Why, certainly, unless it interferes with some plan of Eunice's, and I don't think it will."

I could tell that he was pleased and rather surprised that I had asked him rather than his sister. It occurred to me that perhaps both Eunice and Dale dominated him. A bland, passive man, he would probably have passed his life in some undemanding job—that of an apartment house doorman, say—if it had not been for inherited money and for whatever talent, if any, had produced those cement sculptures.

"Of course, there's the problem of your not having a driver's license."

I said, with dismay, "I never thought of that." Oh, Catherine Mayhew had a driver's license. It was in my suitcase. But I couldn't use it up here.

"It'll probably be all right. Just drive very carefully and stay off the state roads and the interstate highways. Even if you got stopped by the local police, I don't think it would be so bad. I mean, the Andexter name carries weight around here. Besides, I imagine almost everybody has heard about you by now and feels sorry for you."

I knew what he meant. They felt sorry for me because they thought I had lost eight years of my life. But Police Chief George Tate wouldn't feel sorry for me if I were caught driving without a license. He would be only too glad to throw the book at me.

I said, "Isn't there someplace around here called Wrecker's Point?"

"Yes, It's about twelve miles from here, on the ocean."

"I thought I might drive there tomorrow."

"All right. You can get there without driving on main roads. I'll mark an automobile map for you."

"Thank you. And I'll drive very carefully."

He was looking at me with a strange, rueful expression. I somehow felt sure that his thoughts had little or nothing to do with my driving the Porsche. I said, "What is it?"

"What is—I don't understand."

"You were looking at me in an odd way."

"Was I? I didn't mean to. I'll put that map under the door of your room."

"Thanks. See you at dinner," I said and turned away.

CHAPTER 9

A T TEN the next morning I was driving the Porsche along a curving dirt road. On my left was a wall of pines. On my right a sheer cliff dropped away to the blue Atlantic.

I was feeling good. Perhaps part of the reason was that I had had a restful night's sleep. No sounds had disturbed me, even though, before I went to bed, I had seen the tops of pines on the far side of the lawn bending in the wind. But the day's beauty and the car's smooth hum were also responsible for my good mood.

Suddenly I wished I had a right to all this. The car I was driving. My pretty room back in that thick-walled house. The love of that woman with the finely wrinkled face.

But no. Even if it had been possible, I would not have chosen to be Karen Andexter, burdened with the memory of whatever circumstance had caused her flight. Better to be Catherine Mayhew. True, I was alone in the world.

True, the nearest thing I had to a matrimonial prospect was Si Dalyrimple, a man willing to join his signature to a girl's on an apartment lease but not on a marriage license application.

But when I returned to New York it would be with almost ten thousand dollars, a sum which, invested with my friends, might bring me success not only as a shopkeeper but also as an actress. It might even better my marriage chances. It had been my wry observation that the young women least in need of a man's financial support were the ones who reaped most of the proposals.

But it wouldn't be until after Josephine Andexter's expected death that I would go back to New York. I felt a sense of loss at the thought of her dying. But at least her last weeks would have been happy ones. Although she hadn't said so, I'd gained the impression that she was happier now than she had been at any time since fifteen years ago, say, when her granddaughter had begun to move from sunny childhood into troubled adolescence.

Driving slowly and carefully, as I had ever since I left the house half an hour before, I rounded a curve. Up ahead on the right was a turnout. Directly opposite it on the other side of the road, a giant dead pine, bleached to silver, stood beside a granite boulder. Those were the landmarks Brian had told me to watch for. I steered the Porsche onto the turnout, stopped, and left the car.

At the cliff's edge I looked down. I saw steps chiseled in the cliff, leading to a beach strewn with jagged dark rocks. Evidently the tide was in because spent waves washed almost as high as the cliff's base.

Those steps. I pictured Joel Cartwright, laden with tackle, scrambling down them to fish for striped bass.

Better not to think about Joel Cartwright.

I went back to the car, got my beatup old navy blue sweater, spread it on the ground, and sat down. Far out on the water some ship—a fishing trawler? a freighter? —moved slowly past, a black shape against the horizon. Much closer in rose a small islet of jagged rocks. They too looked black as coal against the deep blue water. As I sat there, my thoughts began to drift. The millions of sun sparkles on the sea, winking on and off, had a hypnotic effect. So did the warm sunlight on my face and arms, and the pound and seethe of waves on the beach below.

I don't know how long I had been sitting there when I heard a car's engine. I looked around. A white truck drove in. On its side, painted in black letters, were the words "Cartwright's Garage. Towing, Complete Overhauls." The truck stopped beside the Porsche and Joel stepped to the ground.

Pulses quickening, I stood up. With dismay I realized something. True, I'd stuck to my resolution to stay away from the lake. But without acknowledging it to myself I had hoped that, not finding me at the lake, he would come to the spot he had mentioned to me the day before.

For a moment, saying nothing, we looked at each other through the bright sunlight. Then I asked, "Are you going to fish?"

"Here? No, I caught four trout this morning."

So he must have been at the lake earlier. I said inanely, "It is such a nice day that I decided to drive over here."

He nodded, somber blue eyes fixed on my face.

Nervousness made me blunder. "I was wondering why they call this Wrecker's Point."

He said, after a moment, "You don't know? You really don't?"

I said, dismayed by my carelessness, "Oh, I remember. It had something to do with the rocks on the beach."

"Not the ones on the beach. That group of jagged rocks offshore. Two hundred years ago and more, when shallow-draft ships kept close to the coast, a lantern used to be left burning on those rocks out there."

"To warn ships off?"

He nodded. "But there were wreckers in this area. On stormy nights they would row out, blow out the lantern, and then row back to place lighted lanterns on the beach below the cliffs. Ships' pilots, avoiding the lights they thought indicated that little rocky island, would sail right into it. Then the wreckers would row out to capture what they could of the ships' cargoes."

He paused and then added, "The story is that on stormy nights you can still hear the cries of sailors who drowned out there."

"Oh, yes! I remember now."

A quizzical look in the blue eyes. And no wonder. Karen must have known that legend about wreckers and the ghosts of murdered seamen from her young childhood on. If she remembered anything at all of her life here, she should have remembered something as vivid as that.

I said hurriedly, "It always seemed to me that the story doesn't fit very well with the supposedly upright New England character."

"A lot of things that happen around here don't fit with that idea."

Did he mean his younger brother's involvement with the drug traffic, an involvement he blamed on me? And what did he plan to do about it? Hound me until I decided to disappear again?

I blurted out, "Did you think you might find me here today?"

"Yes, I thought I might."

On summer nights, had Joel and Karen made love, not only in the boathouse, but at this isolated spot?

With him standing only a few feet away from me, I found the idea unsettling. From now on, I resolved, I was going to do everything possible to avoid him.

He said, "I wanted to say something to you. I know we can never be the way we once were. You wouldn't want that, and neither would I. But as far as I'm concerned, we can have a truce. I won't hassle you any more about Danny. When he comes up here, *he* can hassle you, if he's a mind to. But in the meantime, you and I just forget it. Okay?"

"Okay."

"Maybe we could even be friends, or at least not feel we have to keep out of each other's way."

I looked at his face with its strong planes, its mouth with the full lower lip. What would Karen think of him if she met him now, a man near thirty?

I knew what I was beginning to feel about him and it wasn't good, not when I had to keep in mind all the time that I was only a hireling of Eunice and Brian Andexter's, with no real right to anything of Karen's—her identity, her grandmother, or her ex-lover.

I said again, "Okay," and then added, "I have to get back now. I'm having lunch with my grandmother."

I backed the car onto the road, gave him what I hoped looked like a casual wave, and drove off in the direction from which I had come. After about five minutes I turned onto a narrow woodland road which would join the wider one leading to Pinehaven.

CHAPTER **10**

IN MANY WAYS the next two weeks were pleasant. I spent
hours browsing through the library. Evidently no one
had brought a new book into the house in a long time, but
nevertheless I found plenty to read. There were old
friends from my childhood, *The Sword in the Stone* and
Wind in the Willows and *Gone with the Wind*. There
were ancient best sellers I had heard of but never read until now, *Back Street* and *How to Win Friends and Influence People*. Like a glutton at a smorgasbord, I moved
along the shelves in the quiet room, sampling a paragraph of Edna Ferber here and a chapter of J. P.
Marquand there.

I explored back roads in the Porsche, always carefully,
and wandered along woodland paths on foot. During
those weeks, though, I didn't go near the lake or
Wrecker's Point.

At her invitation, I sometimes talked to Eunice while
she painted, either in her cluttered attic studio with its
big skylight or out on the glassed-in porch, with its view

of the rose garden now coming into bloom. Even in the isolation of her attic studio we were careful in our conversation, talking of some TV show we had seen the night before, or of the seedlings which she, aided by Hazzard, had set out in the annual garden.

Hearing her pleasant voice, looking at her handsome head, I wondered what she was really like. Was she as content as she seemed to be to spend her life in this isolated place with her brother, and her lover, and her ancient aunt? Did she know that mild-mannered brother was in one sense her rival? Surely she must know.

But whenever my thoughts strayed in that direction I reminded myself that the relationship of the Andexters with their permanent house guest was none of my business. And anyway, the important thing about them was that they had gone to considerable trouble and expense to bring happiness to the last weeks or months of a grieving old woman.

I seldom had any conversation with Brian except at the breakfast buffet and at dinner and at TV sessions in the library afterwards. But Dale and I played tennis a few times on the court beside the greenhouse. In classic white shorts and V-necked white jersey top he looked dashing indeed. His tennis was not up to his appearance, though, despite a sizzling serve and a pretty good forehand. He had no backhand at all, and at the net he easily became rattled and sent his passing shots wide. He was a good loser, however, almost as cheerful in defeat as in his occasional victories.

It was the hours I spent with Josephine Andexter that I found the most pleasant during those weeks. I enjoyed my lunches with her in her sunny sitting room and I enjoyed her reminiscences. She talked of her travels back in the days when going to Europe involved, not several hours in an uncomfortable airplane seat, but several days aboard a luxurious liner, perhaps with the likes of the Duke and Duchess of Windsor. She talked of somber experiences, too, such as seeing, back in the days of the Great Depression, piles of potatoes on Muskeegan's Main Street. Unable to sell them, farmers dumped the potatoes there for the benefit of the unemployed. Some people, ashamed to admit their need, would wait until the past-midnight hours before filling their burlap bags.

Around three o'clock each afternoon, when it was time for the daily nap Dr. Brawley had prescribed, I would kiss her soft cheek and say, "Until tomorrow, Grandmother." She was that, rather then Josephine Andexter, even in my thoughts now.

I had been at Pinehaven about two weeks when I realized that I needed to shop for such small items as nail polish, pantyhose, and pink wool to mend a sweater I had snagged on a dead pine branch in the woods. When I mentioned the matter, while we were having after-dinner coffee in the library, Eunice said, "Better not drive yourself in the Porsche."

"Of course not." I had no desire to drive into Chief Tate's bailiwick without a license.

"Hazzard can drive you in. But you'll be careful, won't you?"

Careful not to say anything that Karen Andexter, restored to her family after an unremembered eight years, might not be expected to say. "I'll be careful."

In mid-afternoon the next day, as he drove the Bentley along the dirt road through the pines, Hazzard said, "Miss Karen?"

I met his gaze in the rear-view mirror. "Yes."

"Do you know where you want to go in town?"

"Miss Andexter said I will probably find everything I need at Hanson's Variety Store."

"Would you mind if I let you off there and drove on to Cartwright's Garage? I want someone to look at the clutch. It's slipping a little."

I said, after a moment, "Of course you can let me off."

"If they tell me the job will take more than twenty minutes or so, I'll come back tomorrow. I wouldn't want to keep you waiting."

"I won't mind." In fact, after two weeks in that isolated house I would find the bustle of even a small town a pleasant novelty. "I'll take my time shopping. And if you're not at the curb when I come out, I'll have tea someplace. The day we drove in from the airport, didn't I see a cafe called Helen's?"

"Ellen's. Ellen's Sandwich Shop. Nice place. It's been open a couple of years now. It's almost directly opposite the variety store."

"Good. You can pick me up there. And take your time."

Hanson's, I found, was indeed a variety store, selling everything from fire extinguishers to girdles. As I moved along the counters I was aware of curious looks cast in my direction. But no one approached me to say something like, "Hello, Karen. Do you remember me? Dorothy Hines, in grammar school." After I'd paid the cashier for my purchases I crossed wide Main Street to Ellen's. It was a bright, clean-looking place with knotty pine walls and yellow tablecloths. At this in-between hour only a few people, all of them lone women, sat at scattered tables. I chose a table beside the broad front window where I could look out through thin curtains at people moving along the sidewalk.

A thirty-fiveish blond woman, perhaps Ellen herself, was the only person on duty in the outer room. When I'd given my order she went back behind a swinging door, brought out a pot of tea and a cup and saucer, and placed them on my table. She too eyed me curiously, but she said nothing to indicate that she knew who I was. She turned and went back to the cashier's desk.

For perhaps five minutes I sat there sipping tea and looking through the thin curtains. Then I stiffened. A tall man was striding along the sidewalk. I saw him turn in at the cafe's entrance. For a moment he stood in the doorway in blue denim pants and shirt, gaze searching the room. Then he walked to my table.

"Hello, Karen. Mind if I sit down?"

I did mind. My life up here was complicated enough without the unease his steady blue eyes and unsmiling face awakened in me. But I heard myself saying, "All right."

He sat down. When the blond woman walked over to us he said, "Hello, Ellen. Could I have a cup of coffee?"

"Sure thing, Joel."

As soon as she was out of earshot I said, "Did you know I was here?"

He nodded. "Hazzard mentioned it a few minutes ago."

"I—I thought you'd be busy working on the Bentley."

"Someone else is. The business has expanded, Karen. It's not the way it once was, just a three-man operation, my father and Danny and I."

He paused, and then went on, "I figured that if I had

106

to leave college I might as well do the best I could with the garage."

It was because of his father's stroke, I recalled Eunice saying, that Joel had been forced to leave college in his final year.

"I borrowed from the bank," Joel said, "and bought out Kellerman's Garage—it was on the other side of town, remember?—and brought a lot of his equipment to Cartwright's. It's paid off. We have four men working for us now."

And when Danny came back there would be five. Danny the jailbird. I said, "Why did you come here?"

Eyes unreadable, he looked at me for a long moment. Finally he said, "Because at Wrecker's Point that morning we agreed there was no reason why we should avoid each other. And yet you haven't been back to the lake, or to the point, either."

"I've had other things to do."

Although his eyes challenged that, his words didn't. "All right. But will you go fishing with me tomorrow? I'll be down at the lake by nine."

When I just looked at him he said, "I still have that fishing rod you used to use. Will you be there tomorrow?"

"I don't think I can make it."

"Well, try."

He pushed his almost untouched coffee cup away and walked to the cashier's desk. When he had left the cafe I sat motionless for a moment, and then sipped the second cup of tea I had poured from the silver-plated pot. Why, I wondered, did Joel Cartwright want to see me again, at the lake or anywhere else? Was it because he, too, in spite of everything, felt the pull of a physical attraction? Or did he have another reason, one concerned with his long-held bitterness against a girl he once had loved so much?

Movement over in the far corner of the room. A woman was getting up from a table. She must have come in while I was talking to Joel because ten minutes or so ago there had been no one in that corner.

She was moving across the room now, but not toward the cashier's desk. Toward me. After a moment I recognized her. Plump body in a green polyester pant suit. Blond sausage curls. Butterfly-shaped glasses, only now they were dark glasses. Betty Gadsen, Dale Carling's lady friend, or at least one of them.

She said, "Hello, Miss Andexter. Mind if I talk to you?"

Her voice was slurred. It seemed to me grotesque that anyone, let alone a nurse, should be drunk at five in the afternoon in this tearoomy sort of place.

I said, trying to sound welcoming, "Oh, hello, Miss Gadsen. Please sit down."

"Light's too bright here. Why don't you bring your cup back to my table?"

Reluctantly I followed her across the room, placed my cup on the table, and sat down. She said, "I got some Scotch with me. Good stuff. Johnny Walker. You want a spike in your tea?"

Thoughts of Scotch combined with jasmine tea made me queasy. "No, thanks."

She didn't argue, but just added coffee from a pot to the inch or so in her cup. Then she looked toward the front of the room. Evidently the proprietor wasn't watching because the nurse, with a deftness surprising in one tipsy, lifted a pint bottle from a shopping bag on the floor beside her. She uncorked the bottle, poured more than an inch into her cup, recorked the bottle, and restored it to the shopping bag, all within a few seconds.

108

When she had taken a long swallow she set her cup down in its saucer and said, "How's Dale?"

"Why, he seems quite well."

"You sleeping with him?"

I decided that the situation called for pleasant reasonableness, rather than annoyance. "No. We're not interested in each other that way."

She seemed to accept that. Did she have any idea, I wondered, of Dale's relations with Eunice Andexter? Probably not. It would be hard for anyone to associate Eunice's middle-aged handsomeness and cultivated voice and country-gentlewoman air with something as untidy as physical passion.

She said gloomily, "Well, he sure as hell isn't sleeping with me. I haven't even seen him for about ten days now." She took off her dark glasses, and I saw that her hazel eyes were bloodshot and sad. "I want you to give him a message."

"Well, I—"

"Tell him he'd better call me up." Her voice had hardened. "If he doesn't he'll find himself in a peck of trouble." She drained her cup, poured an inch or so of coffee from the pot, reached down again to the shopping bag.

I couldn't keep from saying, "If you're going to work tonight—"

She poured Scotch into the cup, drove the cork home with the heel of her hand. "I'm not." She restored the bottle to the shopping bag. "I've been fired."

"Oh, I'm sorry!"

"It's Dale's fault. He knows it is. I told him so. And yet he doesn't have the decency to even—You see, he thinks I won't have nerve enough to tell anyone. He thinks I'll be too scared of losing him for good, or getting myself into even more trouble—"

She broke off and then said abruptly, "But I'm going to tell *you*. And I want you to tell him I have. He'll realize then that if he drives me to it, I won't be afraid to talk."

"Please! Don't you think you should wait until—"

"You see, I keep a set of keys to the drug supply room in my office. Or at least I *did*," she added bitterly. "Any nurse or even doctor on the four-to-midnight shift had to come to me if they wanted to get into the drug room. I'd unlock the door, go in there with them, and enter in the drug book whatever it was they took out. Then when we left I'd relock the door. When they weren't in use, I kept the drug room keys locked in a drawer of my desk, and the key to the drawer in my purse.

"Well, early last winter Dale started coming to the hospital several nights a week a half hour or so before I was to go off duty. Then we'd go for a drink or two. I loved it, of course," she said bitterly. "I thought his coming there at that hour of the night showed how crazy he was about me.

"One night when he'd been there about five minutes there was an emergency in one of the top floor wards. Some old boy had popped his cork and was rushing from bed to bed, trying to tear out intravenous lines. I hurried up there to see about it. When I came back into my office about twenty minutes later, Dale was reading a newspaper. That was the one time, the only time—I swear to it!—that I left anyone alone in that office with my purse, and with the key to the desk drawer inside it.

"Well, here's the payoff. A few weeks ago they made an inventory of the drug room. They found three hundred amphetamine tablets missing. Some other stuff was

110

gone, too, but only in such small amounts that it might have just been measured out wrong. But three hundred amphetamine tablets!

"I got blamed, of course. Not that I had the only set of drug room keys. Assistant head nurses on the other shifts had them too. But I was the only one who—well, likes the bottle a little too much. I denied that I'd ever been careless with my set of keys. Everything hung fire for a few weeks. Then three days ago they held a hearing, and I got the air. They're not trying to lift my license, but just the same, I may have a tough time getting a job in another hospital."

"And you think Dale Carling stole those pills?"

"I'm a hundred percent sure he did."

"But why? He's no addict."

"No, but he uses drugs sometimes. Uppers every once in a while, and downers, and cocaine if someone else is buying. Because he's also a leech, you see. He liked the idea of getting all that speed without paying for it, just the way he likes living off the Andexters."

"But he's a friend of theirs! And he's helping them manage my grandmother's affairs."

"You think your grandmother isn't rich enough to hire any help they need? He just used that as an excuse. And maybe your cousins like having him around. Or maybe they aren't with it enough to realize he's sponging. Artists are like that, you know. Dreamy."

She looked broodingly at me for a moment and then said, "Will you tell him what I've told you? I want him to realize that if I'll talk to you I may talk to others."

"All right, I'll tell him." It was not that I thought that Dale had stolen those amphetamines. I found it impossible to think of my handsome tennis opponent as

111

overindulging in anything that might spoil his looks. But I felt it was essential that he appease this sorrowful, vengeful woman. Otherwise she might make an open scandal. And then Josephine Andexter, turning in on the local news, might learn that her house guest had been arrested on suspicion of drug theft.

But I could not help saying, "If you have such a low opinion of him, why have you shielded him so far? Why should you care anything about him?"

"Why should I *care?* Look at me, kid. I was no oil painting even twenty years ago. I never dreamed a guy like him would even look at me. You think I want to lose him if there's any way to hang onto him, even if it's for only a little longer?"

"No, I suppose not."

Those bloodshot eyes studied me. "You've changed a lot from the snotty brat you used to be. Maybe it's just being eight years older. But I think it's more than that. I think it must be things that happened to you while you were away."

Feeling more uncomfortable than ever, I remained silent.

"You still got manesia?" Her mispronunciation of the word, as well as the way she leaned forward to peer at me with those sad, bloodshot eyes, made me realize just how drunk she was. "You still don't remember why you left here or where you been or anything?"

"No."

To my relief, I heard footsteps approaching the table. I looked around. Hazzard stood there in his slightly too large uniform.

"The car's ready, miss, if you are."

"Thank you. I'll be out in just a moment."

112

He walked toward the door. I turned back to the woman. "I must go now."

Her hand shot out and imprisoned my wrist. "You'll tell him? You'll tell him I've had it up to here? For his own good, he's got to be warned."

"I'll tell him." I pulled my wrist free. "Goodbye."

Out on the sidewalk, Hazzard opened the Bentley's rear door for me. I was about to step inside when I became aware that a man coming down the sidewalk had stopped in his tracks. I turned and saw Muskeegan's chief of police. He was looking at me with more hatred in his eyes than words could have expressed. I could understand it. He hated me, not just for what had happened eight years ago, but also for his humiliation in Marty's parking lot.

Neither of us said anything. I got into the car and looked straight ahead as Hazzard piloted the Bentley away from the curb. In late afternoon sunlight we drove through the business district and past the scattered houses beyond, and then along the woodland road already deep in shadow.

Just as I entered the house, carrying my purchases, Mrs. Brill emerged from the dining room. She said, "Evening."

Her voice and her round face still held reserve. But compared to what it had been when I first came to this house, her manner was downright cordial. By then I had become aware of just how fond the housekeeper was of her employer. The fact that Josephine Andexter was now a happier woman—and even a healthier one, according to Dr. Brawley—obviously had gone a long way toward redeeming Karen Andexter in Mrs. Brill's eyes.

I smiled and nodded and then asked, "Do you know

where Mr. Carling is?"

"I saw him walking along the downstairs hall in those pretty white shorts of his." It was not the first time she had displayed an animus against the Andexters' permanent house guest. "He had a tennis racket in his hand, so I guess you'll find him out on the court."

I did find him there, hitting yellow balls from a bucket at his feet into the opposite service court. He turned, smiling, as I opened the gate in the court's chain link fence.

"I've been down to Muskeegan."

"I know. Eunice told me you were going shopping."

"I ran into Betty Gadsen in Ellen's sandwich shop."

"Yes?" Still smiling, he began to bounce a ball on the clay surface with his racket.

"She told me—" I broke off, embarrassed, and then resumed, "She told me she thinks you took amphetamines from the hospital's drug room."

His left hand swooped down on the bouncing ball, grasped it. "She told you that?" Surprise and anger in the handsome dark eyes. "She actually told you that ridiculous story?"

"Didn't you know she suspected you?"

"Of course! She told me so. But I didn't expect her to tell anyone else. She must know that I'd be damned sore if she started spreading that silly story."

"I'm afraid *she's* damned sore. She asked me to warn you that if you don't come to see her she's going to tell a lot of people." I paused and then added hesitantly, "Maybe even the authorities."

"The authorities!" His tone was scornful. "Do you think they or anybody would believe I'm an addict? Or that I'm a would-be pusher willing to risk jail for the sake

114

of selling a few hundred amphetamine tablets?"

"No, I don't think anyone who knows you would believe that. But she could cause considerable scandal. And probably my grandmother would hear of it."

It wasn't until after a second or two that I realized I had referred to Josephine Andexter as my grandmother. If Dale noticed, he made no comment.

"I suppose you're right." He'd begun to look worried. He dropped the tennis ball into the bucket. "I guess I'd better go see her right away and quiet her down."

I said, after a moment, "Who do you think took the amphetamines?"

"Good lord, it could have been any of at least a dozen people at the hospital, and maybe more. Everyone knows that nurses and doctors are prone to addiction. They work under pressure, and drugs are always at hand. Of course, it was pretty dumb to take that many tablets all at once, if that's the way they were taken."

"But she says that except for one night when you were there, she always took her purse with her whenever she left her office. And the keys were—"

"I know what she says. But she was coming to work hung over a lot of the time. No telling how often she left her office with her purse still lying on her desk. Besides, the thief may have used someone else's set of keys."

I said, after a long moment, "Dale, I can't imagine why you became involved with such a woman in the first place."

He was smiling again. "Oh, she has her points. And my tastes are what you could call catholic, although not in the religious sense of the word. I can feel attracted to all sorts of people."

That's for sure, I thought.

Aloud I said, "The hospital fired her, you know."

"Yes, I heard. And I really should have gone to her before this." Again his face was sober. "I'll tell her that if she pulls herself together—lays off the liquor, and so on—she shouldn't have any trouble getting a job somewhere else. There's a tremendous nurse shortage. And it might be good for her to get out of town."

Out of town and out of his hair.

What would he promise her? That if she was a good girl, and trotted off quietly to a hospital in some other town, he would still manage to see her frequently? Well, again, none of my business.

"I'm sorry I had to tell you all this, but I thought I'd better." I added, turning away, "See you at dinner."

CHAPTER **11**

ALITTLE AFTER NINE the next morning I emerged from the woods onto the lake's rocky beach. Joel's small boat, its engine silent, rocked gently in the water. At sight of me he turned on the engine and guided the boat to shore. Rubber-booted, he stepped out into shallow water and drew the prow of the boat up onto the beach.

"So you came."

"Yes." I hadn't meant to. I would just take a short stroll down the path through the woods, I had told myself, and then turn back to the house and mend my sweater with the yarn I had bought yesterday. But once headed toward the lake I found myself irresistibly drawn. Oh, perhaps not irresistibly, but with more force than I cared to resist.

"I brought your fishing tackle." Hand on my elbow, he helped me into the boat. He shoved the boat into the water, climbed aboard, and started the engine.

Out in the center of the lake he baited his hook and

117

mine with artificial flies. I said, "I'm afraid I don't remember much about fly casting."

"Remember!" He gave one of his rare smiles. "You never could cast worth a damn. Just don't let the reel run out too far. I don't want to have to climb any more trees to get your hook loose."

For a while we fished in almost complete silence, I making short, awkward casts, he tossing his hook far out in the smooth water and letting the line unwind whistling from his reel. But both his expertise and my amateurishness went unrewarded.

At last he said, "They just aren't biting today."

He removed the flies from our hooks, disjointed the rods, and placed them in a tackle basket. Seated on the thwarts, we faced each other for several uncomfortable seconds. Then he said, "That Bentley's in awfully good condition for a car that old."

"It is? Well, I've always heard Bentleys and Rolls Royces are practically indestructible."

Silence for several seconds. Then I asked, "Do you work on lots of foreign cars these days? I suppose you do."

It went on like that, stilted conversation about cars, and the previous night's TV document on whales, and about two Canadian geese who landed nearby on the lake, kicking up spray as their webbed feet skidded over the water.

His conversation was guarded for reasons I could only guess at. Mine was guarded because I feared that at any moment I might say something that would reveal that until a few weeks ago I had never seen these woods, or the lake, or him.

Suddenly I very much wanted to rid myself of the straitjacket which in New York, in return for a considerable sum of money, I had agreed to put on. I wanted to say, "I'm not your Karen. I'm Catherine Mayhew, an ex-Kansas girl who wants to be an actress but probably will never make it. And I find you far more attractive than is good for me."

But of course I could not say that. For one thing, I could not risk the truth reaching Josephine Andexter's ears. For another, I could not bear the look that would come into his face, a cold scorn for someone who, for money, would deceive an old woman. And never mind that the deception had been meant kindly by the Andexters and by me. The fact remained that it was cold cash that had lured me up here.

And so we went on talking in that stilted fashion. Only once did our conversation veer toward the personal, and then it was at my initiative. I said, "You must have minded leaving college only months before graduation."

"Of course I minded."

"What was your major?"

"Mechanical engineering. I still plan to get my degree. I've managed to put quite a lot aside these past few years, enough to take care of Dad for the forseeable future, and to support myself until I get a degree and a job. I'll just wait long enough to make sure that Danny can run the garage okay. Then I'll take off."

Danny, who'd be getting out soon.

Again silence settled down. Finally I said, "I'd better be getting home if I'm to have lunch with Grandmother." The last word seemed to stick in my throat.

Without a word he started the engine and guided the boat to shore. But when I had stepped out onto the beach he said, "There's a pretty nice dine-and-dance place called Gallagher's, out on Route Fifteen. They have a combo on weekend nights. Would you like to go there Friday night, after the garage closes?"

My pulse beats surged. I heard myself say, "I'd like that."

"Good. I'll pick you up about nine-thirty."

"Goodbye." I turned and walked toward the entrance to the path that led to the house.

Late that afternoon Eunice came to my room and handed me an envelope. Without opening it, I knew that it contained eight one-hundred-dollar bills. I thanked her, then took my suitcase out of the closet, opened it, and placed the envelope beside several similar ones in the suitcase's side pocket.

When I had restored the suitcase to the closet, I said, "Could you sit down and talk with me for a few moments?"

She took the armchair. I sat down on the dressing table bench. "I'm going dancing with Joel Cartwright Friday night."

She surveyed me with suddenly worried eyes. Then she said, smiling, "No need to ask why. He's a very attractive young man in that poker-faced way of his. But do you think you can manage not to slip up?"

"I think so."

"Yes, I suppose you can. And even if you do make a slip, you can always look confused and embarrassed afterward.

"And we don't want you to become discontented up here," she went on. "I know it must seem pretty dull to a New York City girl."

I did not tell her that most evenings in New York the most exciting thing I did was to watch Benny Hill. Like most outlanders she probably was convinced that all

120

young New Yorkers, even those who had to make a living, somehow managed to disco until dawn.

She said, "But if you do go on seeing Joel, what can it lead to?"

I knew what she meant. We had agreed that within a short time after Josephine Andexter's expected death, Karen Andexter would go away for a trip—and not come back.

"It can't lead to anything," I said, "except a very bad scene if he ever learns the truth about me. After next Friday I'll find some way, some *nice* way, to keep him from asking to see me again."

She gave me a dubious look. "That would be best if you can manage it." She got to her feet. "See you at dinner."

Three nights later, Joel's persimmon-colored Mustang carried us through the soft summer dark. Just as the little sport car was in marked contrast to the white pickup truck, so his attire tonight—gray flannels, blue blazer, lighter blue shirt—was a dramatic change from his blue jeans and his khaki shirts and pants. I kept glancing at him from the corner of my eye. His face was tanned from mornings on the lake. As his hand rested on the wheel, I could see a Seiko gold watch showing beneath his shirt cuff. He might have been, not a small-town garage operator, but one of the summer people with houses scattered along the coast who were beginning to appear on Muskeegan's Main Street.

We passed a long stone wall set with a pair of wrought-iron gates. Brass letters on one of the gate posts, illuminated by a spotlight set somewhere in the roadside grass, read, "Muskeegan General Hospital." So that was where Betty Gadsen had worked until her dismissal. I wondered if Dale Carling had been to see her and, in his

121

phrase, quieted her down. Probably. He had been absent from the dinner table two nights out of the last three.

Gallagher's turned out to be a spreading, log-sided structure. Its interior was pleasant indeed, with ample room between the tables, oil landscapes of Maine scenes on the walls, and a fairly large dance floor. The well-dressed clientele seemed to be a blend of natives and summer people. The combo, as if trying to accommodate every taste among patrons varying in age and background, played numbers ranging from country-and-blues to fifties jazz, and from Sondheim to Cole Porter.

We danced and drank and talked. After a while I realized that Joel seemed determined to avoid any reminiscence of years past. Was it because he did not want to risk embarrassing me by bringing up matters which he thought I might remember imperfectly, if at all? Whatever his reason, I was grateful.

A little after one o'clock we started home under a late rising, last-quarter moon. I kept expecting him to stop by the roadside to take me in his arms. When he stopped the Mustang at the foot of Pinehaven's broad steps I was sure he would turn to me. Instead, he got out, went around the car, and opened the door for me. Relieved and yet disappointed, I stepped to the ground.

We climbed the steps. At the door, after I had thanked him for the evening, he said, "Want to try your luck fishing again tomorrow?"

"Why—why, yes." I waited a second or two and then said goodnight and went into the house.

I saw him several times a week after that. We fished, with varying success, at the lake and from the beach at Wrecker's Point. We took a day-long drive down the coast to the New Hampshire border and back. Twice

122

more we went to Gallagher's.

He still did not try to make love to me. I felt mingled relief and resentment, but relief was the stronger emotion. True, sometimes I almost ached to have him draw me into his arms and kiss me. What was more, I sensed again and again that he wanted to do just that. But it must not happen. Once it did, once our attraction to each other swept us into intimacy, I would feel I must tell him the truth. And when I did, I was sure I would lose not only his companionship. That I was already resigned to losing, one way or another, before too long. But I did not want to lose also any respect he might have for me.

And so I went on, happy when I was with him, disturbed and conscience-ridden when I was not. The long June days turned to the almost imperceptibly shorter ones of July. Hazzard's tree roses began to fade, and the beds of annuals he and Eunice had set out came into full glory. And still I had not contrived to do what I knew I should do, and what I had told Eunice I would do—find some graceful way of breaking off my relationship with Joel.

During those weeks I also played tennis several times with Dale Carling. He did not mention Betty Gadsen, but I was sure that he was seeing her. For one thing, he continued to be absent frequently from the dinner table. For another, he seemed relaxed and cheerful. Surely that meant that he no longer feared that she would make trouble for him.

One late afternoon as Dale and I walked back from the tennis court, I asked, "Has Betty Gadsen gotten any job offers?"

"Yes, and she has accepted one of them, at a hospital fifteen miles east of here."

Only fifteen miles away. Its closeness to Muskeegan

123

must have been why she chose that particular hospital.

He said, as if in answer to my unspoken question, "I still see her, of course. No matter what other people think, Betty is good company except when she's had too much to drink."

I was glad she had the job. And I hoped that she would find another man, someone who, unlike the free-wheeling, too-handsome man walking beside me, might become a permanent part of her life.

It was around noon a few days later that Joel said to me, as he drove me home after a morning's fishing at Wrecker's Point, "We just finished repainting our house. Would you like to drive by and take a look at it?"

The Cartwright house was at the opposite end of Main Street from Cartwright's Garage. It was a pleasant, turn-of-the-century house set back on a well-kept lawn. Its fresh white paint, like its bay window, almost sparkled in the sunlight. On its shadowed porch a man sat in a wheelchair.

"There's Dad." Joel angled the Mustang into the curb. "We might as well go up and say hello."

Dismayed, but not knowing how to refuse, I accompanied him up to the porch. The man in the wheelchair, with a blanket covering his paralyzed legs, appeared to be in his middle fifties. Although too thin, his face was still handsome. His eyes, blue like Joel's, also had Joel's disconcerting directness.

"Dad, you remember Karen."

"Of course."

His voice, cold and dry, made his meaning plain. How could he have forgotten Karen, the spoiled rich brat who had played fast and loose with both his sons and landed the younger one in prison?

I said, "How are you, Mr. Cartwright?"

"I'm as you see."

An awkward silence lengthened. At last Joel said, "Well, I'd better take Karen home or she'll be late for lunch with her grandmother."

As we drove toward Pinehaven I said, "I don't think your father liked that very much."

"I know, but I believe he'll feel differently about it once he thinks it over."

"Why should he?"

"Because—you've changed. I think that even in a meeting that brief, he probably sensed that you are different now."

My heart quickened with mingled gladness and dismay. I was important to Joel. Otherwise he really wouldn't have cared what his father thought of me.

And that meant that I must break off with him right away.

CHAPTER 12

THAT NIGHT, lying awake in my room, I made plans. Probably he would be at the lake tomorrow morning. I would go down there and say all the things that constitute the classic brushoff—that I liked and respected him but didn't want to become seriously involved with anyone at the present time. If I had read him correctly, he would be too proud to make any reply to that except "All right. Just as you wish." And, except by accident, we would never see each other again.

The next morning around ten, feeling depressed but determined, I started down to the lake. Earlier that morning there had been a rainfall. It had stopped, but moisture still dripped from the pines to the needle-strewn path. When I reached the beach I saw no boat out on the ruffled gray water and no white pickup truck or orange Mustang standing beside the boathouse. Seated beneath a pine at the edge of the beach, I waited until eleven-thirty. Then I went back to the house. I expected him to phone during the day, but he did not.

The next morning, another gray one, I again went to the lake. He wasn't there. Absurd as it sounds, considering what I intended to say to him, I felt worried and hurt and indignant. Was he ill? Or had something happened to make *him* decide we should stop seeing each other?

By late the next afternoon I still had received no word from him. Despising myself for my weakness, I drove the Porsche to Muskeegan. Again it was raining lightly. My nerves tightened as I passed the cop who, now that the traffic was swollen with the cars of the summer people, presided at the town's busiest intersection. But I did not collide with any car backing out from the curb or make any other error that might have brought me, unlicensed, into the toils of Muskeegan's chief of police. At the far end of Main Street I turned into Cartwright's Garage and stopped beside the gas pumps.

The garage's wide front door was up. In the shadowy depths I could see three men clustered around the grease rack, watching a red sedan rise ceilingward on a huge steel piston. One of the men turned away from the car and walked toward me. For a moment I thought he was Joel. Then I saw that he was an inch or so shorter and somewhat broader in the shoulder. His face, although much like Joel's with its blue eyes and prominent planes, looked about five years older.

It must have been prison, I realized, that had added those years to the face of Joel's kid brother.

For several seconds, while his eyes searched my face, neither of us spoke. Then he said, "Hello, Karen. I heard you'd come back." His voice was neutral, holding neither friendliness nor hostility. I said, feeling grateful for that

127

quiet tone, "Hello, Danny."

"I suppose you want to see Joel."

"Not really," I lied. "I just realized I needed gas. But where is Joel?"

"There's been a bad accident on Route Two-twenty. He went out with the tow truck. Fill 'er up?"

"Yes, please."

I sat there, gripping the wheel, while the gas pump rang six times. Danny racked the hose, took my ten-dollar bill, and went in to the glass-walled office. When he returned with my change he said, "Would you like to go somewhere and talk for a few minutes? There's that diner down the road."

My nerves tightened. Despite his neutral manner, surely he too harbored bitterness against the girl both his father and brother blamed for his imprisonment. But I would have to talk to him sooner or later, and so I said, "All right, if you can leave the garage."

"I can."

He got into the car. Neither of us spoke as I drove through the light drizzle to the diner about a hundred yards away. But when we sat in a booth at one end of the long room, with coffee cups on the table between us and an old Elvis Presley number, "Blue Suede Shoes," on the jukebox, Danny said, "Joel's upset."

I hadn't expected his first words to be about his brother. "Why?"

"He didn't think I'd be out so soon. But the parole board met two weeks early. They moved it up because some of the members were to spend several days testifying before the state legislature."

"But why did that upset—"

"Joel had expected to have more time to think through

128

his problem. About you, I mean."

I said nothing, just waited.

"He's in love with you, Karen." I felt the pulse in the hollow of my throat quicken its beat. "I guess he never fell out of love with you. But he thinks he has no right to feel that way about you. Because of me, I mean."

I managed to say, "I can understand that."

"But I don't feel that way. I never did. Oh, sure, I'd wanted to impress you. And I thought maybe I could if I drove a Ferrari and skiied at Gstaad like Steven. You know, that coke-smuggling brother of one of your friends at that girls' school. But you never actually suggested that I ask Steve to deal me in on the action."

Was that some sort of chivalry talking or was it the truth? Short of finding Karen Andexter and asking her, I probably would never know.

"And anyway, things wouldn't have been so tough for me if I'd just been caught with coke in my car. It was because I hit that cop with a tire iron that they threw the book at me."

I saw sudden bleak humor in his face and knew that he had realized, as I had, that the jukebox was now playing Presley's "Jailhouse Rock."

"What I've tried to tell Joel is that those years in prison weren't so bad. Oh, they were at first." The humor had gone from his eyes, and in its place were memories he probably never would share with anyone. "But later on I got a nice, clean job in the prison library. And I took correspondence courses. If you want to, and if the prison's not too crowded or badly run, you can get a pretty good education while you're doing time.

"Anyway," he went on, "I'm still only twenty-six. I can't say that prison ruined my whole life. In a way, I'm

129

a lot luckier than you. I hear you lost eight years, just plain lost them."

Overwhelmed with sudden guilt, I looked down at the table. Apparently he misunderstood my lowered gaze because he said, "Don't worry. I'm not going to ask any questions about that."

He paused and then went on, "Anyway, I think my coming back here sooner than he expected me to really threw Joel. In spite of all I've said to him, he can't seem to get over the idea that you're to blame for what happened to me. And that puts him in a real bind. He hasn't been near you in the last few days, has he?"

The rain had stopped, but drops of moisture still clung to the windowpane at the end of the booth. Afternoon light striking through the glass cast raindrop shadows on his cheek, so that his face, so much older than it should be, appeared to have dark tears running down it. Suddenly I realized that if I were Joel Cartwright, I too would never be able to forgive Karen Andexter, not fully.

Danny said, "I hope he's at the garage when we go back there. But if he isn't you could still see him tonight. There's going to be a talk—something about tax breaks for small businesses—at Kretchmayer Hall tonight—"

"Where?"

"Kretchmayer Hall, three doors from the post office. I'll write that down for you." He took a business card and a ballpoint pen from his shirt pocket. As he wrote he said, "It's at eight o'clock, and the public is invited. Why not come there tonight? I think the minute he sees you he'll realize he's been acting like a damned fool."

He added, "Sorry about the grease smudge." Before I dropped it into my raincoat pocket I saw that the card

—one of the garage's cards, with "Joel Cartwright, Mgr." in one corner—did indeed bear a greasy thumbprint.

"Thank you, Danny. I think you're a very generous person."

He made a face. "Just because I don't hold a grudge about what happened eight years ago? Hell, we were both just crazy kids."

Yes, but as Joel had pointed out, Karen had been much the older in sophistication. Danny had been a perhaps virginal small-town boy, just out of high school. She had been kicked out of a private school for smoking grass, and she'd already had at least one lover, Joel, and perhaps more. Didn't Danny realize all that? Surely he did. And therefore his forgiving air might be a little too good to be true.

I felt ashamed of myself for doubting his sincerity. Nevertheless, the doubt was there.

Danny said, "Okay if we go now? I shouldn't stay away too long."

When we reached the garage we found that Joel still had not returned. I said goodbye to Danny and then started to Pinehaven under the gray sky.

It seemed to me that Joel's not being at the garage was some sort of sign to me, a sign that I should carry out my decision of a few days earlier to break off with him. Of course, there might be no need. Perhaps Joel already had resolved to stay away from me from now on. But I certainly would not go to that lecture tonight or make any other effort to see him.

Feeling as dreary as the sky overhead, I left the Porsche in the garage, walked back along the drive, and entered the house through a rear door. Mrs. Brill stood at the hall table, holding the phone to her ear. She said into the

131

mouthpiece, "Here she is now." She handed the phone to me and then walked away down the hall.

Nerves tensing, I knew who the caller must be. "Hello."

"Hello, Karen. Will you meet me at Wrecker's Point in half an hour?"

I waited until Mrs. Brill disappeared through the kitchen doorway. Then I said, "Why, Joel?"

"I'll tell you when you get there."

Heart beating fast, I considered. Better to see him now, right now, while my renewed resolve to put him out of my life remained strong. "All right." I hung up and walked back along the drive to the garage.

As I drove over little-used roads to Wrecker's Point, I rehearsed what I would say. It seemed to me that I should express more than a reluctance to become seriously involved. Instead I should say, "Talking to Danny this afternoon made me realize just how heavily the past weighs on both of us. I don't think we could ever be really comfortable with each other, even as friends."

When I was about half a mile from the Point, the near-setting sun dropped below the curtain of dark gray clouds into a strip of serene blue. Sudden radiance flooded the dirt road, the pines, the Atlantic stretching away from below the cliff at my right. Moments later I saw that Joel had already parked his white pickup truck, dyed pinkish by the strange light, on the turnoff at the point. As I steered the Porsche off the road, he got out of the truck.

He opened the door for me and I stepped down onto the sparse grass. For a moment we looked at each other silently and unsmilingly. In that sunset light his face looked Indian bronze. I managed to say, "What is it you—"

132

"Danny told me about that talk he had with you this afternoon. He's right, you know. I do love you, far more than I did eight years ago."

I found I could say nothing at all. Then, as I just stood there, he reached out for me and drew me close. His warm mouth with its full lower lip covered mine in the kiss I had wanted for weeks.

When he lifted his head he looked down at me with those steady blue eyes. "Will you marry me?"

I ached to say "Oh yes!" But after that? After that I would have to say, "By the way, I've been deceiving you all these weeks." And so I said nothing at all.

"We could go to New Haven. Now that Danny's here, he can take over the garage."

"New Haven?"

"So that we could get settled before I enroll at Yale for my final year. I've got enough to support us both until I graduate."

Then, his voice flat: "Is it that you don't love me? I thought you did."

I cried, "Of course I love you!"

His arms tightened around me. "Then marry me."

"Please, Joel! I have to think."

"What is there to think about? We love each other. Why shouldn't we marry?"

It occurred to me to say, "Don't you see? It's those missing years. I could even be married to someone else." But I couldn't say a miserable, lying thing like that, not when my lips were still tingling from the pressure of his.

"Please!" I said again. "Let me think it over."

He gave me one of his rare smiles. "All right, darling. Will you come down to the lake tomorrow morning?"

"If—if I've thought things through by then."

133

We kissed again, this time with my arms tightening rather desperately around his neck. I got into the Porsche. When he had closed its door he leaned down and said, again with a smile, "Think real hard."

I did try to think hard, all the way back to Pinehaven and all through the dinner I shared with Brian and Eunice. (Dale Carling again was absent.) I tried to think while we had coffee in the library, with tiny figures on the TV screen, unheeded by me, acting out some sort of documentary about Winston Churchill. I still tried after I went to my room.

It was almost midnight when, as I lay in bed, I stopped trying. It was no use. My thoughts kept going in circles. What I needed was at least a day or two away from this place. And I needed to talk to someone, someone for whom I could lay out the whole problem.

Si Dalyrimple.

He was intelligent and clear-headed. And, in addition to an amiable letch for me, he seemed to have a genuine liking for me. Surely he could help me to sort things out.

Nor would he hold a grudge because I had withheld the facts until now. Before I left New York I phoned to tell him that I had answered the *Village Voice* ad and that I had been hired by people who ran a summer theater in Maine. I had made no mention of the name Andexter, or even of the town of Muskeegan. Remote as the chance was, I could not risk Si turning up in Muskeegan and asking around for Catherine Mayhew, "the girl some people named Andexter brought up here." In no time at all the news would have reached that gentle old woman, turning all her newly found happiness into renewed and even more bitter grief.

134

But I would lay the whole problem before him now and trust him not to do anything to hurt the woman for whom I had come to feel so much affection.

The trouble was that he traveled frequently, down to the Atlantic City casinos, or to various racetracks, and sometimes to Florida for the dog races. It would be best to phone his apartment right away, before I made more plans to go to New York. I had no fear of disturbing him. Even when home for the evening, he stayed up until all hours.

Use the extension in the upstairs hall? No, I might awaken someone. Best to use the phone in the library.

I hauled my suitcase from the closet, opened it, and rummaged in the side pocket where I had placed my bank books, charge cards, and anything else that could identify me as Catherine Mayhew. I found my address book. Yes, I had remembered Si's phone number correctly. I replaced the suitcase and put on my robe.

The amber wall lights in the upstairs hall and the chandelier in the lower hall, its globes dimmed, lighted my way down the stairs and back to the library. I switched on a table lamp, lifted the phone from its cradle, dialed. He answered on the second ring.

"Si, it's Catherine."

"Cathy! When did you get back to town?"

"I didn't. I'm still up in Maine."

"How you doing up there in the boondocks? Laying them in the aisles?"

"Si, listen. I'm coming to New York and I want to see you."

"Sure, sweetie. When are you coming?"

"Tomorrow. I'll fly to Boston from an airport near here

135

and then take the shuttle to New York."

"Tomorrow! Hey, I'm sort of—Wait a minute. I'll check."

He was gone from the phone for several minutes. When he came back he said, "Just as I thought. My calendar's jammed. But look. I'm due at a party tomorrow night, people named Hartsdale. Why don't you meet me there around eight? We'll duck out as soon as we can and go to a bar or someplace, and then you can tell Papa all about it."

"About what?"

"About your troubles. Your voice is full of trouble, love. Got something to write on?"

"Yes."

"Here's the Hartsdales' address."

There was a pad of note paper and an attached pencil on the desk. I took down the address. It was in one of those gentrified neighborhoods on the lower West Side, a former slum where newcomers had restored many of the old houses. "Thanks, Si."

"See you tomorrow night."

We both hung up. After that I called the small airport about five miles from Muskeegan. A night employee finally answered, in a voice so drowsy that I knew he must have been sleeping on the job. The first plane left for Boston at seven-thirty, he told me, and got there in time for an early shuttle to New York. I left the library.

I was partway up the stairs before I saw the tall figure on the landing, silhouetted against the dim second-floor lights. After a startled moment I realized it was Eunice. As I drew close she said, "I thought I heard a voice downstairs. Is anything wrong?"

I said, after a moment, "No, I just wanted to tele-

136

phone, and I thought I might disturb someone if I called from upstairs."

"Called? Called whom? Something is wrong, isn't it?"

I had no intention of telling her I intended to confide in Si, a man she didn't even know. That was sure to alarm her. And so I said, "I was calling the local airport. I want to go to New York tomorrow."

"New York!" Then, as I started to speak: "Wait. We'd better go into your room."

I had left the light on there. She sat on the dressing table bench and I on the bed's edge. Even in a blue flannel robe and with a net over her smartly groomed hair, she looked poised and dignified. She said, "Why do you want to to to New York?"

I decided to be frank about that. "I need to think something through, and I believe that I can look at the situation more clearly if I'm away from here, if only for a brief time. You see, Joel Cartwright wants to marry me."

After a moment she said, "I'm not surprised. You've been seeing a great deal of each other." She paused. "How do you feel about him?"

I said wretchedly, "What difference does it make? I couldn't marry him without telling him the truth. Even if I didn't tell him, he'd find out before long. And think what he'd feel then!"

"All right. Tell him you don't want to see him again."

"I don't think that would keep him away." Not after I had kissed him there in the sunset light and told him I loved him.

"Then why not stall him? After Aunt Jo is—is no longer with us, you can just disappear for the second time, or so it will seem to him.

"What you can't do" she went on, her voice very firm,

137

"is walk out on Aunt Jo. You can't break her heart all over again. Not now."

I said dully, "No, I wouldn't do that. Don't worry. I'll be back in a couple of days at most. I won't even take my suitcase with me, just a shoulder tote."

"Where will you stay?"

"Some hotel."

"As soon as you register, will you call me up? Otherwise I'll worry."

"I'll call you."

"What time do you have to be at the airport?"

"Seven-thirty."

"All right. Hazzard will drive you there."

$\mathbf{A}$ROUND SEVEN the next evening I gazed down through the sealed window of my hotel room at Lexington Avenue, four stories below. Even though the room behind me was air-conditioned, I could tell it was still very hot down there in the street. The people on the opposite sidewalk, moving in the gray light filtering through an overcast, had what I had come to think of as a July-in-New-York look, an expression of stoic endurance but with rage lurking just underneath, ready to lash out at any pedestrian who jostled them or at any driver who encroached upon the crosswalk.

My hotel room was second-rate or perhaps even third-rate, with a spot here and there on the beige carpet and a wash basin tap in the adjoining bath that kept trickling no matter how hard I tried to turn it off. But I had balked at the thought of paying ninety or a hundred dollars for a hotel room. The sixty I had been charged for this one seemed to me outrageous enough.

Through the window's double thickness of glass I heard the grind of metal against metal as a taxi cut in between another taxi and a bus. Fists waved, and mouths twisted with imprecations I could not hear. It seemed to me almost unbelievable that about twelve hours earlier I had been moving through that house deep in the Maine woods.

Knowing that Josephine Andexter always awoke very early, I had gone to her room as soon as I had finished dressing that morning. I found her breakfasting in bed from a wicker tray that held a pot of tea and a rack of toast. When I told her that I was going to New York "to shop" for a day or two, I saw what I had feared to see, a leap of sheer terror in her eyes.

"Oh, no Karen! What if—what if—"

"I have a loss of memory again? But I won't, Grand-mother. I feel very strong in every way. And I do need warm-weather clothes. The things at Hattie Eager's in Muskeegan are sort of—"

"Tacky is the word you are looking for, my darling. But couldn't you go to Augusta, say?"

"If I go that far, why not go to New York?"

"I suppose so. But a young girl like you—"

I forebore to point out that I could no longer be considered a young girl. She added, "Won't Eunice go with you?"

"Eunice is working very hard on a large painting. Now don't worry, darling. I'll be back safe and sound before you know I've gone."

I kissed her, went back to my room, and packed in my brown leather shoulder tote the few things I would need for a brief stay in New York. From the side pocket of my

140

suitcase I transferred five one-hundred-dollar bills to my handbag.

Half an hour later, with Hazzard at the wheel, the Bentley carried me along the pine-bordered dirt road and through the little town. Even at this early hour Muskeegan seemed fairly wide awake, with both cars and pedestrians moving along Main Street. As we passed Ellen's Sandwich Shop I saw George Tate, who must have been breakfasting, emerge onto the sidewalk, a toothpick projecting from his lips. He looked hard at the Bentley, but whether or not he could see that it was I who sat far back in the passenger seat I don't know.

We passed Cartwright's Garage. I did not see Joel, of course. With a pang I realized that soon he would be driving to the lake, almost certain that he would find me there. Danny, though, was at the garage, feeding gas into the tank of a gray sedan. He looked at the Bentley as it passed, but again I didn't know whether or not I had been recognized as the old car's passenger.

At the little airport I said goodbye to Hazzard. The flight to Boston was brief and the one to New York only a little longer. With no luggage to wait for, I was able to catch the first airport bus into town. The air was sweltering and the sky gray, promising a rain that might cool the city off for at least a little while. I was glad that at Pinehaven that morning I had decided to wear my raincoat.

At the terminal, feeling a bit superior to all those tourists waiting in line for taxis, some of which would take them to the Ambassador by way of New Jersey, I traveled swiftly by subway to Sixty-eighth and Lexington and walked into the Hotel Mardon. The desk clerk turned the register toward me. I had nearly completed my signa-

141

ture before I realized that I was registering as Catherine Mayhew. Well, it really didn't matter which name I signed.

A bellhop brought me to this room. As soon as he was gone I dialed Si's number. One of those answering devices expressed his regret that he was out and asked me to leave my name and message. I said that I was Catherine, that I had just arrived at the Hotel Mardon, and that I would see him that evening. Then, as I had promised, I phoned Eunice and told her where I was.

I napped briefly—my sleep the night before had not been sound—and then freshened up in the bathroom with the ever-flowing tap. At six I had gone down to the hotel's coffee shop for a bacon-and-tomato sandwich. According to the radio tuned low behind the counter, rain was expected. I had returned to this room and stayed in it, reluctant to brave the heat until absolutely necessary.

Now, standing at the window, I looked at my watch. Seven-ten. I put on my raincoat and took the elevator down to the lobby.

Since this was that in-between hour, with the home-going rush over and the theater rush just starting, I had thought I would have no trouble getting a taxi. But in the sweltering street I found that I was wrong. At least a score of taxis passed me, their roof lights either extinguished or showing the off-duty sign. Finally I turned toward the subway entrance. At this hour, with the cars still fairly full, I had no qualms about traveling underground. And after I emerged at the Fourteenth Street and Eighth Avenue stop, surely I would be only a short walk away from the address Si had given me.

I caught a local. The car, while not crowded, had a

reassuring number of passengers. At Fifty-ninth Street, and later at Grand Central, the car remained fairly full. But as the train traveled southward, wheels shrieking, it grew emptier at each stop. Finally, as the train approached my transfer point at Fourteenth Street, there were only four other passengers in the car—an old woman who sat with a shopping bag propped between her arthritic-looking knees, two tall, bearded blacks in jeans and cotton mesh sport shirts and dark glasses, and a small man of indeterminate ethnic background who wore stained and baggy brown trousers and a frayed blue shirt, and who stared at me unwinkingly.

Perhaps those weeks in Maine had sensitized me. Anyway, I found myself increasingly aware of the stupid but somehow menacing obscenities spray-painted on the walls, and the steady stare of the small man, and the unseen eyes of the black men. Useless to tell myself that the blacks were probably Columbia University students, and the small man one of the thousands of annoying but harmless ex-mental patients whom the hospitals have released to roam the streets and subways of New York. My nerves remained taut and my palms damp.

When the doors slid open at the Fourteenth Street stop I remained seated for a second or two and then moved quickly out onto the platform. I turned around to watch the doors close. The blacks still sat motionless, and the other man still stared at the space I had vacated. The train pulled out.

Feeling a little foolish, I threw a quick glance around the almost empty platform, bathed in that cold, feeble light that illuminates subway stations and bad dreams. A sign above the platform indicated that I was to climb a

143

flight of stairs to reach the Fourteenth Street line. I did so, aware of the echoing sound of my own footsteps on the metal treads.

At the top of the stairs another sign directed me to turn right. A few yards farther on I saw still another sign telling me to descend a second flight of stairs. I did so, hand moving along the iron rail.

A rush of footsteps behind me. I started to turn, but something—a metal bar, the side of a karate-chopping hand?—struck me below my left ear. Darkness closed in, but not before I was aware of pitching forward toward the cement platform below.

CHAPTER **14**

FOR A WHILE after that my consciousness was like a defective movie film, showing brief scenes interspersed with blank stretches. I recall a young policeman's face—transit police, city police?—bending over me. Then a blank stretch. After that a swaying motion and the howl of a siren. Then again blankness until I was lying on a table of some sort, and a dimly seen man, with an Asiatic face above his white coat, was shining a light into my eyes.

My last memory of that night is of a young nurse propping me up in bed with one arm. "Better take this sleeping pill, Miss Andexter."

Andexter? Oh, yes. But how did she know that in a small Maine town hundreds of miles away I was known as Karen Andexter?

When I awoke my mind felt confused and sluggish. Even so, I somehow knew that there would be no more blank stretches in my consciousness. Hazy sunlight came through the window at an early morning angle,

145

streaming across my hospital bed and almost touching the empty one a few feet away.

A nurse, a middle-aged one, poked her gray-blond head around the door and then came to stand at the foot of my bed. "How are we feeling this morning?" The question was routine enough. The curiosity in her eyes, I felt, was not.

"Fairly well, except my head aches. The rest of me does too, a little."

"That's mostly shock, although you do have a few scrapes and bruises from falling down those subway steps. Your main injury was concussion, but even that's not bad. You should be out of here by tomorrow."

"Where's here?"

"Bellevue Hospital. You were brought in around eight last night."

"What happened to me?"

"You were mugged, apparently, but your purse wasn't taken. Maybe something or someone frightened the mugger off. Anyway, you still had your purse with more than three hundred dollars in it and no identification."

So that accounted for the curiosity in her eyes. No identification. All the identification I possessed—bankbooks and credit cards and driver's license, all made out to Catherine Mayhew—was in my suitcase at Pinehaven.

No other identification at all. And yet that young nurse last night had called me Miss Andexter. Or had that been some sort of hallucination?

While my sluggish mind was still wrestling with the problem, the woman at the foot of the bed asked, "Are you up to seeing a visitor? I mean, you won't have breakfast for another half-hour. Of course, it isn't visiting

146

hours yet. But the poor man has been waiting here since five this morning."

Si. It couldn't be anyone else. When I didn't show up at the party, he must have phoned the hotel and learned that I had left some time before. Growing alarmed, he had called the police. And he had been waiting somewhere in this hospital since five. I felt both grateful and surprised. Such concern for anyone seemed to me incompatible with Si's cheerfully self-centered character.

I said, "Oh, yes. Please send him in."

She left me. Only a few minutes later he was standing tall in the doorway, his face pale under its tan, his blue eyes both weary and anxious. He smiled and walked toward me.

Joel. The last time I had seen him had been at Wrecker's Point, with radiance streaming from beneath the cloud curtain in the west onto his face. And here he was in a New York City hospital room.

He pulled an aluminum-framed chair close to the bed and sat down. "How do you feel?"

"I'm fine," I said idiotically. "Joel, how on earth did you know I was here?"

"The hospital phoned the garage around closing time last night. They described you and then asked me who you were. I told them."

"But I still don't see—"

"They found one of the garage's business cards in your coat pocket."

I remembered then. The booth in the diner. Danny Cartwright scribbling on a card and then handing it to me, with an apology for his greasy thumbprint.

"As soon as I hung up," Joel was saying, "I called the

147

local airport and then the one in Boston. Jim Harper —he's a friend of mine at the Muskeegan airport— said he would fly me to Boston, but the remaining flight from there to New York was booked up. So I decided to drive, starting right then."

He must have driven all night. No wonder that his eyes were tired and that his face, pale under its tan, had a muddy look.

Suddenly I loved him so much that I wanted to cry. I said, "You must be exhausted."

"Driving at night isn't so tough. Very little traffic. A few hours' sleep today will fix me up. I've already booked a room at a motel on the West Side.

"And it's a good thing I drove down," he went on. "You and I can have a nice drive back." He paused. "You planned to come back, didn't you?"

"Yes."

"Why did you come down here?"

I looked at him helplessly, wanting to say, "I came down here to try to decide what to do about you." I couldn't say that because I still hadn't decided. Oh, I loved him, now more than ever, but that would make it all the harder to confess that I had been deceiving him all these weeks.

He said, "Don't get upset. You don't have to answer that if you don't want to."

An attendant, a red-haired girl with glasses, came in with my breakfast tray. Joel stood up. "I'm going to get some sleep now, but I'll be back later today." He bent and kissed my forehead and then left.

When I had finished breakfast I went back to sleep for a while. I awoke still feeling stiff and sore. My headache

148

was much better, though, and my mind no longer felt clouded. Just before noon a plainclothesman who appeared to be near retirement age came into my room, introduced himself as Sergeant Somebody-or-other, and sat down beside my bed.

"I'd like to ask a few questions. First, I want to be sure we've got your name spelled right."

He looked at me expectantly. If I'd known that a policeman might turn up, it would have been different, but as it was it took me a moment to realize what name he meant. "Karen Andexter," I said and spelled it for him.

"Address?"

"Rural Route Four, Muskeegan, Maine."

"Can you describe the perpetrator?"

"The—? Oh, the person who struck me. No, I didn't even see him."

"Well, since you lost no property and you're not badly hurt, I guess I won't bother you any longer."

Soon after the policeman left a youngish doctor—a white man, rather than the Asiatic of the night before—came in to shine a small light in my eyes and ask me if that bruise on my neck hurt. Until then I hadn't known I had a visible bruise there. "You're doing fine," he said. "You ought to be able to leave tomorrow morning."

Within minutes after the doctor left, the phone rang. It was Eunice. "My dear girl! How are you?"

"Pretty much okay. But how did you—"

"Joel Cartwright phoned us last night as soon as the hospital called him. We phoned the hospital right away, of course, and they told us you weren't badly hurt. I

149

called again this morning, but they said you were sleeping, and so I waited until now. Are you sure you're all right?"

"Bruised and a little concussed, they tell me, but otherwise okay. You haven't told my—You haven't told your aunt anything about this, have you?"

"Of course not!" She paused and then asked, "Is Joel there?"

"In New York, you mean? Yes. He came by car. I'll drive back with him, probably tomorrow."

She was silent for a moment. I knew she must be wondering what I had decided to do about Joel. But all she said was, "Well, make sure he drives carefully. We'll be anxious until we have you safely back here. I'll phone you early tomorrow morning."

We said goodbye and hung up. I stared at the ceiling, considering. It would be best to phone Si. For one thing, surely he was wondering why I hadn't shown up at the party. For another, I wanted him to collect my shoulder tote from the Hotel Mardon and pay my bill there. It was the only way I could think of to make sure that Joel did not learn that I had registered at the Mardon as Catherine Mayhew.

I dialed, hoping that I would not have to talk into one of those recording devices. I did not have to.

"Dalyrimple's Wet Wash. Where shall we pick up your bundle?" He often answered the phone with the name of some fictitious laundry, taxidermist, or similar establishment.

"Si, this is Catherine."

"Cathy mine! How come you stood me up last night?"

"I got mugged."

150

"Now there's a good reason. Did you get hurt? You don't sound hurt."

"Not badly. Enough that they took me to Bellevue, but they're letting me go tomorrow morning."

"Some welcome back to New York, huh? Did he get much loot?"

"None. He didn't even take my handbag."

"After going to all the trouble of mugging you? That's typical of what's happening to this country. Slackness, all down the line. Look, sweetie, I'd come down and sit beside your bed of pain, but I'm up to my pectorals in work. Besides, you'll be out tomorrow."

"That's right." Nevertheless I felt more than a little miffed by his light-hearted reaction to the attack upon me. And here for a few minutes that morning I had pictured him sitting anxiously in the hospital's waiting room.

I went on, "But if you're going to be anywhere near the Hotel Mardon today, would you do me a favor?"

"Oh, yes, the Mardon. You mentioned it in the message you left on my phone recorder. Sure. I'll be going up to Fifty-ninth and Lex pretty soon, and that's not far from the Mardon."

No need to wonder what he would be doing at Fifty-ninth and Lexington, the site of Bloomingdale's. To the outrage of that famous emporium, its potential customers sometimes bought from sidewalk vendors who were supplied by Si Dalyrimple and who displayed their wares a few feet from the store's entrance.

"Will you pay my bill at the Mardon? I'll mail the money later. And will you collect my shoulder tote? It's in my room, still unpacked."

"Sure, but what do I do with it?"

151

"Could you have someone drop it off at the main desk here at the hospital?"

"No problem."

"You can leave a note with it saying how much I owe you. And one more thing."

"Yeah?"

"Address the note to Karen Andexter and tell at the desk that it is Karen Andexter's luggage."

He said, after a moment, "What's up, girl? You using an alias? You, whom I always considered a veritable June Allyson, complete with little white collar and little white soul. This I've got to hear about. Maybe I'll come to the hospital, after all."

"No, don't come. I'll tell you all about it someday."

It was ironic, considering that I had come to New York for the express purpose of laying my problem before Si, but now I felt a sudden distrust, an unwillingness to tell him anything at all or even see him. I could not say where that distrust had come from, but it was there.

"Okay, mystery lady. But you'd better run that name by me again. And spell it."

I did. We talked for a few moments more and then hung up.

Soon after my dinner tray had been removed that evening, Joel came in. He said, "You look much better."

"So do you." His eyes appeared rested, and his face no longer had that muddy color.

"They tell me you can check out at ten tomorrow. Do you think that you'll feel up to starting back to Maine then?"

"I'm almost certain I will." About forty-eight hours after I left, I would be starting back to Maine with my problem still unsolved and nothing to show for my trip

152

except a few bruises. But after that experience on the subway, I could not help but feel glad to be going.

He leaned over and kissed me, on the lips, this time. "Sleep well."

Shortly after noon the next day, with New York City well behind us, we were traveling through a bright sunlight along the interstate highway through Connecticut. Joel slowed the car, turned off onto a paved rest stop, and switched off the engine. I said, with surprise, "Anything wrong?"

"Yes." His level gaze rested on my face. "I want to know who you are."

CHAPTER 15

STUNNED and speechless, I looked at him.

"You're not Karen Andexter. I've been fairly sure of that for some time now. So who are you?"

"What—what makes you think—"

"Look. To save us both time, I'll tell you right off the bat how I know. It's the way you talk."

"The way I—"

"Oh, not your accent. You've got that down pretty pat. One would think you were a born downeaster. And although I don't know how you manage it, you even sound like Karen, or at least the way I remember her sounding."

Miserably silent, I thought of the hours I'd spent listening to that recording Karen had made for her grandmother.

"But when you've been running a garage for a few years," he went on, "you learn how to tell what part of the country various people come from, not just by their license plates or their accents, but by the way they pronounce place names. Missouri, for instance. Maybe you don't realize it, but you say Missoura. Midwesterners do that. And then there are regional expressions. Once when you and I talked of spending a whole day at Wrecker's Point, you said, 'I'll ask Mrs. Brill to put some sandwiches and fruit in a sack.' In the Midwest they use that word instead of bag."

He paused, but when I said nothing he went on, "And when I kissed you for the first time the other evening, I was doubly sure you were not Karen. I can't say just how I knew. But it was different, so different that even a lapse of eight years could never have accounted for it. So tell me who you are. What's your name?"

Numb and helpless, I told him.

"Where were you born?"

I told him.

"And how is it that you've been passing yourself off as Karen Andexter?"

Here it was, the question whose answer might mean the loss, not just of his love, but his respect. "Brian and Eunice Andexter hired me to pretend I was Karen."

"Hired you? For how much?"

"Eight hundred a week." I forced the words out. "They—they guaranteed me pay for twelve weeks, even if things turned out so that I could leave earlier."

"Things?"

"I mean, even if their aunt died before the twelve weeks were up. That's why they hired me. They wanted the last few weeks or months of their aunt's life to be happy ones."

"But you'd never even met Karen's grandmother, had you?"

155

"No."

"So it wasn't to make her happy that you went up to Maine, was it?"

"No, it was for the money."

Stumbling over my words, sometimes stopping entirely until a question from Joel got me started again, I told him of my futile efforts to get somewhere in the theater and of my growing distaste for my life in New York. I told him how I had wanted to take up my friends' offer of a one-third share in their loft apartment and their dress shop and how the Andexters' proposition seemed to guarantee that I could.

"Yes, I did it for the money. But once I got up there and met Karen's grandmother—well, I've come to love her as if she were *my* grandmother. I don't expect you to believe that, but it's true."

"What do you mean, you don't expect me to believe it?"

As I looked at him, bewildered, he went on, "Of course I believe it. I've been able to tell how you feel from the way you talk about her. You couldn't have faked that."

He paused and then said, "If I'd thought you were capable of faking a thing like that, I wouldn't have been able to love you."

It took several seconds for his words to sink in. I heard myself make an inarticulate sound, a kind of joyful whimper. He drew me close to him and kissed me.

Head on his shoulder, and feeling the sting of tears in my eyes, I looked through the windshield. A few feet beyond the front bumper was a large green refuse container of corrugated metal. Overloaded, it had spilt paper plates and cigarette wrappers and a banana peel onto the

156

asphalt. I felt a shaky smile on my lips. The loveliest moment of my life so far had occurred within a few feet of a trash can.

Joel said, arms still around me, "I'm not hurting you, am I? Your bruises, I mean."

"No." And even if he had, it would have been more than worth it.

He stroked my hair. "One thing more. Why did you go to New York?"

"I had to decide what to do. You'd told me you loved me. I knew that I couldn't go on seeing you without telling you the truth, and yet I was terrified that it would make you despise me. And so I went away to try to make up my mind."

"But why New York?"

"I have a friend there, Si Dalyrimple. I thought he might advise me."

"And did he?"

"No. As it turned out, I never even saw him. I was on my way to meet him when I was attacked there in the subway." I paused and then went on urgently, "And you won't tell anyone in Muskeegan that I'm not Karen? Anyone at all? If Josephine Andexter learned the truth, it would be a terrible blow, worse than even her first loss of her granddaughter."

"I'll tell no one, not even my father or Danny." After a moment he added, "Well, we'd better get moving."

We drove on through the golden afternoon, across valleys where rivers glinted in the sun, and over gentle hills that gave us views of distant villages, each with its white-spired church. Around six we were traveling through New Hampshire's more rugged terrain. On a

157

level stretch, Joel turned onto the roadside grass.

"We had best stop for dinner soon."

"Yes."

"And after that? Shall we stop someplace for the night?"

"Yes." It was an answer, not just to his spoken question, but also to the one in his eyes. He kissed me, and then we drove on.

After midnight few cars moved along the highway that ran past the motel. Even though we'd drawn the draperies back, the sound of car engines came only faintly through the floor-to-ceiling plate glass windows into the darkened motel room. Sometimes, though, as Joel and I lay there in the quiet aftermath of love, the glow of headlights wheeled through the room and across his bare shoulder.

He said, into the silence, "Then you'll marry me as soon as you can?"

I knew what he meant. As soon as a loving old woman's death freed me from pretending to be her granddaughter.

"You know I will."

His arm tightened around me. Again he was silent for a while. Then he said, "How many people knew you were in New York?"

I said, surprised by his abrupt change of subject. "Why, Si Dalyrimple, of course. In fact, he knew ahead of time that I would be there because I phoned him from Maine. And I suppose everyone at Pinehaven knew."

"Anyone else?"

"I imagine anyone who saw me ride through the town in the Bentley that morning could have found out. Seeing me headed in that direction at that early hour they could probably assume I was going to the airport, and it would have taken only a phone call to check. But why? Why do you ask?"

"That mugger. He keeps bothering me."

"Joel, I don't understand."

"Why didn't he take your handbag?"

"I suppose because something or someone frightened him off. What other explanation could there be?"

"Suppose he wasn't an ordinary mugger. Suppose he had some other reason."

"What reason? What are you talking about?"

"Darling, don't get upset. In all probability you just got mugged, as scores of people do in New York every day. It's just that you were struck down almost as soon as you ventured out of that hotel—"

Abruptly he broke off and then said, "But we can decide all that later. Let's not waste time talking now."

He leaned over me and kissed me. For a while after that we didn't talk at all.

When Joel stopped the Mustang at the foot of Pinehaven's front steps the next day, Eunice came out to meet us. Although usually undemonstrative with me, she put her arms around me and kissed me.

"How are you, Karen? I mean, *really*?"

I was glad I had thought to turn up my raincoat collar to hide the bruise on my neck. Although by now it bothered me scarcely at all, it had turned a shocking color, blue and green and purple.

"I'm fine. Does—does she—"

"Aunt Jo knows she'll see you soon. We told her about your phone call this morning."

159

I had telephoned around eight, before we had breakfast as the motel.

She turned to Joel. "I guess I don't need to thank you for bringing her back."

"You don't." A smile tugged at his mouth. "It was my pleasure."

"You'll stay for lunch, of course. It's at one. Karen usually has lunch with her grandmother, but perhaps today—"

"Thank you, but I'd better get to the garage as soon as possible." He turned to me. "Goodbye for now, Karen."

Karen. But his eyes were reminding me that it was Catherine he had held in his arms the night before. He turned away.

Eunice and I went inside. She said, "Brian is out in his studio and Dale is someplace in the village, but you'll see them both soon."

"Fine."

I went up to my room. I had just divested myself of my raincoat and shoulder tote when someone knocked.

It was Mrs. Brill. "So you're back, are you? Maybe next time you'll decide Muskeegan stores are good enough for you and not go running off to that—that jungle."

It was the nearest thing to an expression of concern I had ever heard from her. "It feels good to be back, Mrs. Brill."

"Your grandmother's awfully anxious to see you."

"And I can't wait to see her. I was just about to go to her room."

"Better cover that bruise with a scarf. No one's told her about your getting into trouble down there, you know."

"I intended to wear a scarf."

She started to turn away and then said, "I made

chicken pies for lunch."

Another mark of goodwill. Mrs. Brill's individual pies —flaky crust over poached chicken and tiny onions and green peas in a delectable cream sauce—were my favorite concoctions.

"Wonderful!"

"I'll send it to your grandmother's room, along with plain poached chicken for her."

When I entered Josephine Andexter's sitting room a few minutes later, she held out her hands to me, and joyful tears sprang into her eyes. "So you're back!"

"You knew I would be."

"Yes, of course! It's just that after all that time when you were—away, I can't bear to have you out of my sight for long."

She broke off and then said, "Bring your chair close and tell me all about your shopping trip. Did you buy a lot of pretty things?"

"Not a lot. I didn't see much I liked." It would be best, I realized, to buy a couple of Hattie Eager's dresses as soon as possible.

She said, as if catching part of my thought, "Well, Hattie Eager's shop is all right, at least for summer things. And heaven knows the poor woman needs all the customers she can get. Her husband left her with nothing but debts, you know."

That made me realize how out of touch Josephine Andexter was, here in her sun-flooded suite. Hattie Eager, I had heard, had gone to Arizona five years ago to live with her brother. The present "Hattie Eager" was her nephew, whose wife and daughter waited on customers. Well, in a way, her being out of touch was all to the good. It minimized the chances that news of anything

161

disturbing—my experience in New York, for instance—would ever reach her.

She and I passed an even more pleasant than usual three hours. After lunch I read aloud to her for a while from an Edith Wharton novel, *House of Mirth*, about New York society early in the twentieth century, and that led her to reminisce about Bar Harbor, a resort at its fashionable height during her girlhood. At three o'clock Dr. Brawley arrived, and so I went to my room.

About forty-five minutes later I went down to the library to see if it contained Edith Wharton novels not on Josephine Andexter's shelves. I was climbing the stairs with *Ethan Frome* in my hand when I saw Dr. Brawley descending.

"How is she, Doctor?"

"Remarkable. In the past few weeks her blood pressure had gone down, her heart rhythm has steadied, and even her cholesterol level is down. It's being happy that does it. You're better for her than any amount of medicine."

"I'm so very glad." The doctor's words made my deception of her seem more than justified.

Around five Eunice came to my room. She said, seated in the armchair, "What have you decided to do about Joel Cartwright?"

I had an answer ready for that, of course. "I've decided just to leave things as they are now." Learning that Joel knew the truth about me would alarm Eunice greatly. *I* was sure that Joel would keep his promise to tell no one, not even his father or brother. But I could scarcely expect her, who knew him mainly as a tradesman a generation younger than herself, to repose equal faith in him.

"You mean, you have given him no definite answer to his marriage proposal?"

I said, hoping my words carried conviction, "It seemed best not to."

She nodded. "I know you must hate to deceive him, and to keep him dangling. But it *is* best to leave things as they are as long as Aunt Jo—as long as she needs you."

At dinner that night Brian and Dale listened attentively to my account of my misadventure in the subway. Brian asked, "Do you know what he hit you with?"

"No. The side of his hand, perhaps. The hospital said my main injuries came from falling down those stairs. So maybe he wanted to hurt me just enough to be able to get away with my handbag."

Dale said, "But you told us he didn't take your handbag."

"Maybe he got rattled. Or maybe he wasn't a thief. Maybe he was just someone practicing his karate chop."

"I'm glad you can joke about it," Dale said. "But I've heard that after the evening rush hour those subway stations south of Grand Central are apt to be pretty empty. You should have taken that into consideration."

"After this I will."

Around ten, after I had undressed and turned out the light, I walked to my bedroom window. On the opposite side of the broad lawn the pine trees stood motionless as a child's cutout against a sky strewn with stars. Joel and I had arranged to meet at the lake tomorrow morning. It would be beautiful there.

New York with its shrieking sirens, its hit-and-run criminals, might have been on another planet. I turned away from the window toward my bed.

CHAPTER 16

T
HE NEXT TWO WEEKS were pleasant indeed. Joel and I
spent a few hours together almost every day at the lake,
or at Wrecker's Point, or, in the evening, at Gallagher's.
Twice Danny accompanied us to the dine-and-dance
place. His subdued and yet amiable manner was much as
it had been the rainy day we sat in the diner near the
garage. I had needed no assurance that Joel had kept his
word not to tell his brother who I really was. But if I had
needed such proof, Danny's unaltered manner would
have supplied it.

At that New Hampshire motel, Joel and I had agreed
that from then on we would not give full rein to our
desire for each other. It was unthinkable, of course, that
we make love in that boathouse where young Karen had
lain in his arms. Joel never even suggested it. Nor did we
want to go to any of the motels near Muskeegan. It was
not just that I feared word of it might reach Josephine
Andexter. I sensed that Eunice and Brian also might not

like it. And as a matter of fact, I shrank from being even more talked about than I had ever since I came to Maine. It was bad enough to read speculation in the others' eyes about what had happened to Karen Andexter during the eight years of her disappearance.

While I was getting dressed one morning about two weeks after my return from New York, I tuned my transistor radio to a broadcast of local news from the small station in Muskeegan. After speaking of a minor fire at the Muskeegan hardware store the night before, the announcer said, "Local friends of Miss Elizabeth Gadsen will be shocked to hear of her untimely death. Late yesterday Miss Gadsen, forty-eight, was found dead in the bedroom of her garage apartment in Hoving Springs. Her landlady, Mrs. Marie Wiley, discovered the body. Not having seen Miss Gadsen depart for work, Mrs. Wiley went out to the apartment to investigate.

"At the Hoving Springs County Hospital, the cause of Miss Gadsen's death was listed as a cardiac arrest.

"For many years she was a nurse at Muskeegan Hospital. Early this summer she left her position here and joined the staff of the County Hospital.

"Internment will be in Albany, New York, Miss Gadsen's birthplace. She is survived by a brother and two sisters, all residents of that city."

Strange that the news disturbed me so much. After all, I had met her only twice. Perhaps it was because the depth of her sadness was so obvious, a sadness I had hoped she might escape by taking another job and by putting at least a little distance between herself and the man she loved but could never hope to possess more than fleetingly.

Of late Dale had been having breakfast at about the

165

same time I did, but that morning he was not in the dining room. I wondered if he had heard about Betty Gadsen.

When I finished breakfast I went out to the tennis court. Dale was there practicing his serve, smashing ball after ball from the bucket beside him into the diagonally opposite service court. When I walked through the gate in the high fence he turned toward me.

I said, "Did you have breakfast early?"

"I didn't have it at all. I felt too upset."

"Then you heard the news broadcast."

"About Betty? Yes. It was a shock. I saw her only a week ago, and she seemed fine then. I thought she was finally paying attention to my lectures about her drinking, but maybe not."

Frowning, he bounced a ball up and down on his racket. "I know she was just a middle-aged lush. But believe it or not, I feel pretty damned awful about her dying all alone like that."

He tossed the ball high and smashed it across the net. I turned and walked down to the lake to meet Joel.

Half an hour later, with the small boat's engine turned off, we floated on blue water almost as smooth as glass. Joel too had heard of Betty Gadsen's death. "In fact, I heard of it last night from the county sheriff. He came in to have his brakes tested."

"Did he have any news that wasn't on the radio this morning?"

"A little. That landlady gave a statement to the police, of course. She said that she woke up in the night and heard voices in the garage apartment, but she thinks it may have been one of those all-night radio talk shows."

Dale, I recalled, had implied that he had last seen

Betty a week ago. But it could have been someone else in her apartment, perhaps that nice, obtainable man I had hoped she would meet.

I thought of her sad, bloodshot eyes and her lonely death. Then I looked at Joel, my beloved who loved me, and I thought of the years stretching ahead of us.

Well, as someone has remarked, life is unfair.

July gave way to August. Summer people became more numerous on the village street, and sometimes even in that north country the days were uncomfortably warm. Occasionally there were utterly still nights when not even my open windows brought sufficient air into my room. Since Josephine Andexter and I were the only occupants of that wing of the house, I felt it was all right to try to create a small draft by leaving the door to the hall slighty open.

It was on such a still night that someone else died, someone far closer and dearer to me.

I don't know what it was that awoke me. Perhaps a vaguely unpleasant dream about something—a seal? a small whale?—washing up on the rocks below Wrecker's Point. I was moving toward it when I woke up. Or perhaps it was some sound that aroused me. (The next day I was to wonder if Josephine Andexter, in her final extremity, had managed to cry out to me in some telepathic fashion.)

I got out of bed, went to that slightly open door, and looked out. The dimly lit hall stretched emptily away in both directions. Drowsily aware that my room was cooler now, I closed the door and went back to bed. Soon I was asleep.

At the usual time, around eight, I woke up. I had

167

gotten out of bed and put on my robe when someone knocked.

"Come in."

It was Mrs. Brill. She closed the door behind her and then stood there, her plump face so wretched that I knew instantly what had happened. For several moments grief tightened my throat so that I could not speak. Then I said, "When?"

"Sometime after midnight, Dr. Brawley says. It was Edith who found her, when she brought in her breakfast tray."

I asked numbly, "Did Dr. Brawley say it was her heart?"

She nodded.

"He's still here?"

"No, he left about seven." Her face crumpled. "Oh, Karen! She seemed so much better. I had begun to hope—"

Her tears started my own. We walked toward each other and stood embraced, weeping. At last she said brokenly, "You've got one thing to comfort you, child. You've made her so happy this summer. If you could know what she was like those years you were gone, that sorrow always in her eyes even though she seldom mentioned you— But you came back, and so—"

She broke off. Sound of shuffling footsteps in the hall. Mrs. Brill and I looked at each other and then moved toward the window.

An ambulance down there at the foot of the broad steps. Then two white-coated men descended to the driveway, carrying a stretcher between them. We watched as the mortuary vehicle carried away all that was mortal of Josephine Andexter, who once danced with

168

Edward the Eighth when he was still Prince of Wales. Josephine Andexter, whom I had loved almost as much as if she really had been my grandmother.

Three afternoons later, a bright day with drifting small white clouds, I stood with twenty or thirty people around the open grave in the Episcopal churchyard. While a tall young clergyman read the beautiful and ancient phrases of comfort from the Book of Common Prayer, I suddenly found myself thinking, not of the dead woman, but of her granddaughter. I had an eerie sense of Karen Andexter's presence somewhere nearby. The feeling was so strong that, as I looked across the many headstones to the pines that walled the churchyard in, I almost expected to see her standing among the trees, a blond young woman with a face that could have been my sister's, perhaps even my twin sister's. I saw no one, of course.

The young minister closed the prayer book. As I moved with the other mourners toward the churchyard gates, I heard the first clods of earth fall on the coffin. Then Dr. Brawley was walking beside me. "Are you all right, Karen?"

"Of course." Then I burst out, "But you told me she was so much better."

"She seemed to be. Blood pressure, heart action, even muscle tone had improved over the summer. I'd begun to hope she would last for years longer. She came from long-lived parents, as I'm sure you know. Both her father and mother lived past ninety-five. But even young people, apparently in perfect health, can die suddenly, and so it isn't surprising that she did."

He took my hand and patted it. "Just be glad that you were able to give her that happy summer."

"I am glad, terribly glad."

169

I went through the churchyard gate and got into the old Bentley with Brian and Eunice and Dale. About a dozen of the Andexters' oldest friends followed the Bentley back to the house, where red-haired Edith moved about the living room serving sherry and small sandwiches. Their stay was mercifully brief. When we had seen the last of the guests out the front door, Eunice said to me, "Would you mind coming into the library for a few minutes?"

In the silent room, with the door into the hall closed, Eunice and I sat down on the leather sofa that faced the unlighted fireplace. She said, "I know you must be eager to resume your own life. And we told you that your —your position here could end when Aunt Jo died. But could you spare us a few more weeks? We'll pay you for them, of course."

As I looked at her questioningly, she went on, "Brian and I have been here fifteen years, you know. In that much time you accumulate a lot of things. I've got to sort through them, deciding what to discard and what we should take with us. Neither Dale nor my brother is good at tasks like that. Dale is too impatient, and Brian too slow and absent-minded."

I said, bewildered, "But where are you going?"

"Back to Bangor, of course. Already a friend there is looking for a place for us to rent."

"But why? This is your house now."

"Oh, no, my dear. This house, and all the land around it, and all but a little of her cash estate goes to the Open Land Conservancy."

"The what?"

"The Open Land Conservancy. It's an environmental organization. You see, until Karen disappeared, Aunt Jo intended to leave nearly everything to her grand-daughter. But when she finally gave up hope of Karen's return, she made a new will leaving Karen's share to the Conservancy. Brian and I were left the same amount in the new will as in the old, fifteen thousand a year apiece."

"Fifteen thousand a year!" During my weeks here I had come to realize that Josephine Andexter was a very rich woman indeed. I was shocked that she should leave such a paltry sum to her niece and nephew.

"You mustn't think badly of Aunt Jo for that," Eunice said. "In the first place, she had been out of touch for many years with such matters as inflation. To her, fifteen thousand a year must have continued to seem like a very respectable sum. Besides, Brian and I have income from what our father left us. And then we make some money from the sale of our work."

Precious little money, I imagined. All the time I had been here, neither of them had mentioned making a sale.

"But the main reason she left all that money to the Conservancy," Eunice went on, "was that she feared that Pinehaven might end up as a ski resort."

"Ski resort!"

"Yes. A number of companies have offered several million. They'd turn the house into the main lodge, with additional cottages scattered through the woods and ski lifts running up Old Blue. I guess she had some sort of assurance from Karen that that would never happen. But once her granddaughter disappeared, she decided to leave the bulk of her estate with the Conservancy just to make sure that the land and house would be preserved as they are."

I could understand that. She must have hated the

171

thought of strangers crowding the house where she had been happy with her husband and her son, and where her beloved granddaughter had grown up.

A sudden thought struck me, a dismaying one. "But perhaps she changed her will again this summer. After all, she thought that she had her granddaughter back again."

Eunice shook her head. "Certainly she did nothing about it when you first came here. She neither went to see her lawyer, Harold Ponsby, nor had him come here. And she couldn't have consulted with him since the middle of July, even if she had thought of doing so, because Harold Ponsby is in Nova Scotia. Even though he's in his forties, he spends two months back-packing up there each year. He won't be back until the middle of September.

"His being away will delay the probate of the will, of course. But the Conservancy knows they are the chief heirs. Their representatives will be in this house as soon as it is legally possible, making sure that Brian and I don't carry off anything that doesn't belong to us. I'd like to have all our things sorted out by that time. Will you stay and help?"

I could scarcely refuse a plea like that. Besides, there were practical reasons for consenting. Joel and I, once we were in New Haven with rent to pay and furniture to buy, as well as all his college expenses to meet, might find good use for the additional money Eunice was offering me.

"I'll stay."

"Thank you." With a weary gesture she ran her fingers through her graying brown hair. "And one thing more. Until you're ready to leave, will you go on letting people think you are Karen Andexter? I don't think I can cope

172

right now with the sensation it will cause in the village and with all the explanations we'll have to give."

I too dreaded the speculation the news would cause. "Some New York soap opera actress, huh? Well, I never! They say that Eunice and Brian Andexter hired her at a whopping salary just to make the old lady happy. But I wonder how much the girl got out of the old lady herself? A few diamonds, maybe?"

In fact, I had dreaded such talk so much that Joel and I, down at the lake the morning after Josephine Andexter's death, had agreed that there was no need to let Muskeegan know the truth about me until after I left. We were going to do it the easy way. We would meet in New York or New Haven and get married. Only then would he write or phone the truth to his father and Danny and perhaps to a few friends. The news would of course spread. But by the time Joel and I returned to Muskeegan—for Christmas, say—time would have robbed the story of much of its sensation.

I looked at Eunice Andexter's weary face. Should I tell her now that Joel already knew who I really was? No, no point in giving her an additional cause for anxiety when she already had so much on her mind.

She sighed. "Well, I'm glad I'll have your help. Now I think I'll lie down for a while before dinner."

CHAPTER **17**

A SENSE OF LOSS weighed upon most of my waking moments during the next few days. When I was with Joel I could sometimes forget for a little while. But as soon as I entered that house I was reminded that never again would I lunch with her in that sunny sitting room and hear her stories of a time when both she and the century were in their teens. Remembering how she and I used to giggle—yes, actually giggle—over some old photograph, or a note written to her by some swain back before the First World War, I would get the feeling that this household had lost, not an elderly woman, but someone young and blithe.

Joel and I saw each other every day, usually down by the lake. In the afternoons, though, I helped a harried-looking Eunice prepare for her move back to Bangor. We spent hours going through silver and china stored in sideboards and the butler's pantry. We spent more hours, hot and dusty ones, up in the enormous attic, sorting

174

through everything from old magazines to clothing.

One late afternoon about a week after Josephine Andexter's death, I had just finished washing the attic dust from my hands and face when someone knocked on the door of my room. It was Edith.

"Miss Karen, Miss Andexter wants you to come down to the library as soon as you can."

When I entered the library a few minutes later I found not only Eunice but also Brian and Dale seated around the unlighted fireplace, Eunice on the leather couch, the two men in flanking armchairs. Mrs. Brill stood beside the white marble mantel. I caught the impression that despite the lingering grief in her face she was quite pleased with herself.

"Shut the door, please, Karen." Eunice's voice was tense. "And then come over here."

It was not until I sat down beside Eunice that I saw the papers on the coffee table in front of her. There was an official-looking document with a blue cover, ripped in half. Beside it lay a plain white sheet of paper covered with writing that I instantly recognized as Josephine Andexter's. I had seen that neat, small handwriting many times in old photograph albums and diaries we had leafed through.

I became aware of an electric tension in the room. No one spoke for a few moments. Then Eunice said, "Two weeks ago your grandmother made a new will. Mrs. Brill found it just this afternoon."

"I've been going through her things," the housekeeper said, "and this afternoon I got around to her dressing table. I found the torn-up old will and the new one in a drawer. I don't know why she put it there instead of her desk. She seemed bright as a button most of the time, but

175

every once in a while she'd do something odd like that."

I waited, gaze fixed on the papers on the coffee table.

Brian said, "Her new will leaves everything to you."

I cried, after a stunned moment, "But that can't be! After all—"

Eunice's hand shot out and gave mine a warning squeeze. "Oh, Brian didn't mean everything. There's a nice bequest to Mrs. Brill, larger than in the old will, and also bequests to Hazzard and Hannah and Edith. And she's increased the yearly sums Brian and I are to receive by five thousand more dollars each, which is very nice. What Brian meant was that you have been left everything that under the destroyed will would have gone to the Open Land Conservancy."

I said, still stunned, "You say she drew it up two weeks ago?"

Eunice said, "That's the date on it."

"But how could she if her lawyer wasn't here?"

"Oh, she consulted Harold Ponsby's secretary. We found that out when we called Ponsby's office a few minutes ago. Aunt Jo asked her to destroy the copy of her old will, which is in Ponsby's files. Aunt Jo destroyed her own copy and then made that new will in her own handwriting."

"She must have had some sort of premonition, poor darling," Mrs. Brill said. "She figured she had better not wait until Mr. Ponsby came back."

I cried, "But a will like that can't be legal!"

"A holograph will?" Dale Carling said. "It's the most legal kind there is because every word of it is in the deceased's handwriting."

I stared, aghast, at that document by which Josephine Andexter had meant to make me a multimillionaire.

176

When it came out that I was Catherine Mayhew, how could I ever convince most people that I had not come here with the fraudulent intent of inheriting Josephine Andexter's fortune? Why, I might even find myself on trial.

I heard Eunice say, "Thank you, Mrs. Brill. I know you must have other things to do now."

When the door had closed behind the housekeeper, I waited for a moment and then asked in a low, urgent voice, "What in God's name shall we do?"

"Nothing, for the moment," Eunice said. "We'll wait until Harold Ponsby gets back and take his advice."

"This will can't be submitted for probate!"

"And it won't be. Ponsby will straighten things out. In the meantime, we just do nothing."

"Could I look at the will?"

"Of course."

I skimmed through it. She had begun by stating that this was her last will and testament and that it superseded any previous wills. She had left a lump sum of twenty-five thousand dollars to Mabel Brill and smaller sums to each of the other servants. In a separate paragraph she left twenty thousand dollars a year apiece to Eunice Andexter and Brian Andexter, "not only because they were my dear husband's niece and nephew, or because they have assisted me for many years, but more importantly because they helped restore to me my granddaughter, Karen Andexter."

Tears blurred my vision as I read, "Everything else I possess I leave to my dear and beloved granddaughter."

There was a final sentence denying the Open Land Conservancy any part of her estate. Then she had written down the date.

177

I laid the paper back on the coffee table. "Don't look so upset," Brian said. "You've done nothing wrong." And Dale added, "Hell, no. You gave her something that maybe no one else on earth could have given her. And as for this mess about her will, Ponsby will straighten it out as soon as he gets back and we lay all the facts before him."

The next day broke gray and rainy. I knew that even if the sky cleared, Joel would not be at the lake. He was scheduled to go to the county courthouse in Hoving Springs. The prosecution had subpoenaed him to testify in the trial of a man who had brought his car to Cartwright's garage after it allegedly had been involved in a hit-and-run accident.

Eunice, who often breakfasted in bed, came down to the dining room that morning looking very country-gentlewoman in a beige sweater of lightweight wool and a beige-and-gray checked skirt. "I'm going into town to the bank and to do some shopping. Probably I'll be away most of the day."

"Is there anything I can do while you're gone?"

"You might keep going through those stacks of old magazines in the attic. Just place to one side the ones Brian and I have subscribed to, *Arts Monthly* and *Painters and Sculptors*, and so on. We'll decide later how many of them we will take with us."

When the Bentley had carried her down the drive, I decided that this was no morning to spend in the musty attic, with the gray light made even dimmer by the dust film on the windows. Instead I would go through the book stacks in the library and take down the ones that had Eunice or Brian or Dale Carling's name on the

178

flyleaf. When I had suggested several days before that we sort out the books, Eunice had said, "Let's tackle that later." But there was no reason why she should mind if I began the task now.

In the silent library I pushed the little wheeled stepladder up to the shelves lining the space between the fireplace and one wall. I would look through the entire top shelf on that side of the room, I had decided, and then work my way down. No need to look inside the leatherbound sets of Hazlitt and Dickens and Goethe and many other classics. I already knew that they bore the bookplates of John Andexter, Josephine's husband. In many books dating from the twenties, thirties, and forties I found Josephine Andexter's small, neat signature on the flyleaf. But both Brian and Eunice also had placed expensive art books on these shelves. And Dale Carling, evidently far more of a reader than either of them, had written his name on the flyleaves of novels by Ian Fleming, and books on tennis, and military history, and—surprisingly—Japanese wrestling.

It was around ten when I found, close to the fireplace on the bottom shelf, a book entitled *Hazardous to Your Health*. I had a vague memory of reading reviews of it. Published several years before, it had been still another of those muckraking attacks on the medical profession. Mildly curious, I pulled the volume out and, seated on the low stepladder, started to open it.

It fell open of itself at a point midway of the book. Evidently some person frequently had opened the book to those pages and perhaps even left it lying open face down.

I started reading the paragraph that began near the top of the lefthand page:

179

Not many people realize it, but there is one potentially deadly drug that quite literally disappears once it is introduced into the human body. It is the muscle relaxant succinylcholine. A white powder, it is dissolved in water and then administered by hypodermic needle. Within the body, it rapidly breaks down into two substances, succinic acid and choline, both of which are normally found in human tissues. In short, the succinylcholine has vanished without a trace!

A highly useful drug, small quantities of it can relax a patient's muscles during abdominal surgery, say, so that the surgeon may operate more easily. But too much of the drug will cause widespread paralysis of *all* muscles, including those which enable the body to maintain breathing movements. The result of course, is death.

One wonders how many patients who die on operating tables supposedly of cardiac arrest, are in fact the victims of some careless anesthetist.

Even more disquieting is the thought of succinylcholine as an undetectable murder weapon. As everyone knows, the tiny puncture mark left by a hypodermic needle can be almost invisible if the injection is made in the groin, the armpit, or inside the mouth. One wonders how many thousands of physicians, making out certificates of death due to "cardiac arrest," have been unaware of such punctures. And if later on some relative or friend, growing suspicious, demands an autopsy, the murderer is still safe because the deadly poison had long since broken down into two harmless substances found in every human body.

I turned to the flyleaf. No signature at all. But on the inside flap of the book jacket was a small sticker bearing the words "Lighthouse Bookshop, Bangor, Maine." Bangor, where Eunice and her brother and Dale Carling had first become friends.

I turned to the page bearing the publishing date. It was 1980. Perhaps Dale Carling had brought this book with

180

him when he joined his friends at Pinehaven. Perhaps Eunice or Brian had bought it during a trip to Bangor. Perhaps they had ordered it to be sent to them by mail. In any event, it was unreasonable to think that anyone except one of those three could have brought the book into this house.

I reread part of a sentence: "One wonders how many thousands of physicians, making out certificates of death due to 'cardiac arrest—' "

In the last few weeks, Betty Gadsen and Josephine Andexter had both been pronounced dead of cardiac arrest. And the night Josephine Andexter had died, something had awakened me. The sound of a person or persons moving down the hall past the door I had left open an inch or two? The sound of an old woman's feeble cry a second before someone clapped a hand over her mouth, and someone else plunged a hypodermic needle—

Terrified and sickened, I told myself to stop imagining such nonsense. The heart of a middle-aged alcoholic had worn out. So had the heart of a woman in her mid-eighties. Neither death was at all surprising.

And another thing. It was possible that, if she had gone on making threats, Dale might have wanted to silence Betty Gadsen. But what possible reason could he or either of the Andexters have had to hasten Josephine Andexter's death? To obtain the yearly sum she had willed them? That was absurd. Here in this mansion staffed with four servants, and with unlimited access to such amenities as two expensive cars and a tennis court, they had lived on a far grander scale than the money she had willed them could provide.

My thoughts swerved back to Betty Gadsen. What was it she had said about those missing drugs at the hospital?

181

Oh, yes. Besides the amphetamines, small amounts of other drugs had been missing.

What if the amphetamines had been stolen merely to distract attention from the loss of those other substances?

Again feeling sick, I wondered if one of those drugs could have been succinylcholine.

Well, there was one way I could try to find out. I could ask Oren Wisart, director of the Muskeegan Hospital, who had attended Josephine Andexter's funeral—which was only appropriate, considering that she had paid for an entire wing of the hospital. Surely he would feel obligated to allow her granddaughter to ask a few questions. And I would go to him right now. If he could assure me that neither succinylcholine nor any similar substance had been missing from the hospital's drug room, maybe I could dismiss these ugly thoughts.

The rain had stopped, but apparently Dale still considered the court too wet for him to practice his serve as he usually did before lunch each day. As I walked back to the garage I saw neither Dale nor Brian, but only Hazzard and the young teenager who helped him with the gardening chores. They were trundling wheelbarrows, laden with potted begonias from the front terrace, toward the greenhouse. It made me realize that it was already September first, with the start of the long Maine winter not far away.

I drove the Porsche into town, too upset to care very much whether or not I was stopped by Chief Tate or one of his minions. As I passed the garage I saw Danny Cartwright. Back turned to me, he stood beside the window of a car, talking to its driver.

At the hospital's reception desk I was directed to the

182

third floor. I found a door marked Oren Wisart, Director. A pretty blond secretary said, "Just a moment, Miss Andexter. I'll see if Mr. Wisart is free." She flipped a switch, spoke briefly into the telecom, and then smiled at me. "Mr. Wisart will see you now."

In the inner office a large, well-barbered man with graying blond hair rose smiling from behind his desk and waved me to a chair. When we were both seated he said, "I want to tell you again how much I sympathize with you in your loss. In fact, it is the whole community's loss. Your grandmother was a wonderful woman."

"Thank you. I thought she was too."

"Now what can I do for you?"

"It concerns Elizabeth Gadsen when she was an assistant head nurse here. I wonder if I could ask a question of two."

"Certainly." But his eyes had become wary.

"She told me about amphetamine tablets that had disappeared from the hospital drug room. She also mentioned that small amounts of other drugs were missing." I paused. "Could you tell me if one of the drugs was succinylcholine, or some drug with similar properties?"

"I couldn't answer that offhand. I'd have to consult the records." But his eyes, not just wary now, but alarmed and angry, had already answered it.

"However, it really doesn't matter what drugs they were because only minuscule amounts had disappeared. Slight errors in measurement could have accounted for the discrepancy."

"I see."

He hesitated and then said, "I hope you didn't pay too much attention to anything Miss Gadsen told you. She

183

was an excellent nurse for many years, but by the time we had to ask for her resignation, she had become—most unstable."

"I gathered that."

"Nothing is more important to a hospital than its reputation. Your grandmother would have been the first to be distressed by rumors about the hospital being—well—careless in its handling of drugs."

"Oh, I realize that. And I have no intention of spreading rumors."

"I'm glad. And I'm glad that I have been able to tell you that, except for the missing amphetamine, nothing of any consequence has ever happened to the hospital's drug supplies." He glanced toward the window. "Oh, look. The sun is breaking through."

We exchanged a few trite remarks about how brief New England summers were, and yet perhaps all the more pleasurable because they didn't last long. Then he said, "Do you mind my asking why you came here today with those questions?"

I had my answer ready. "Well, I read about muscle-relaxant drugs in a novel, and I wondered if there really were such things. Then I thought of what Betty Gadsen had said, and so I decided to come here and ask."

From the look in his eyes I knew that I had gone down in his estimation. What a spoiled, silly creature, I could imagine him thinking. Something she's read in a book piques her idle curiosity, and so she comes here, taking up my valuable time—

He said, "Well, I'm glad I could be of service to you."

"Thank you," I said and got to my feet.

So that I would not have to talk to Brian and Dale at lunch, I stopped at the diner halfway between the

184

hospital and Cartwright's Garage for a sandwich. As soon as I reached the house I went to my room and stayed there until the dinner gong sounded.

The table conversation that night was prosaic enough. Eunice talked of her shopping trip. Later on she and Dale got into an argument over, of all things, school prayer, with Dale saying that prayer "might help keep some of those young rowdies in order," and Eunice replying that no one with an ounce of religious feeling would want to use prayer as a disciplinary weapon "like rules to hit children over the head with."

I looked around the candlelit table at those three middle-aged people, all handsome, all with an air of self-assurance and good breeding. Conspirators? Murderers? Nonsense!

And yet there were the two deaths, and the look in Oren Wisart's eyes when I mentioned succinylcholine, and the sound, or whatever it was, that had awakened me the night Josephine Andexter died.

What was more, I suddenly realized, there had been that attack upon me in the almost empty New York subway station. One of the three of them could have done that. Which one? Dale, undoubtedly, since he was the youngest and most athletic of the trio.

They knew I had registered at that Lexington Avenue hotel because, true to my promise, I had telephoned Eunice soon after I got there. Dale could have waited somewhere near the hotel entrance until he saw me come out and then have followed me into the subway. Standing at the door of the car next to mine, he could have seen me emerge onto the platform at the Fourteenth Street stop—

But why should he have made that frightening but not too damaging attack on me? To keep me from talking to

Si Dalyrimple? I hadn't even told Eunice that I intended to talk with Si, or anyone. Besides, I could have talked to him the next day at the hospital if I had chosen to. Then why? Why the attack? To make sure that I didn't linger in dangerous and dirty New York, but instead rushed back to the peaceful Maine woods?

But that still left the chief question unanswered. If the three of them had conspired, what had they gained, or hoped to gain?

After dinner, unwilling to spend more time in their company, I pleaded a headache and went to my room. The next morning, encountering Eunice in the upstairs hall, I said that I still was not feeling well and asked to be excused from working in the attic.

"Why, of course! As a matter of fact, I won't be up there either. I intend to paint today."

At seven Joel arrived to take me to dinner at Gallagher's. Reluctant to spoil the evening, I said nothing at the restaurant about my anxieties. But on the way home I told him of Mrs. Brill's discovery of the holograph will.

"Joel, she left almost everything to me—or to Karen, that is."

"Oh, Lord!" he groaned. "I suppose we should have expected her to do something like that, but I never even thought of it. Did she ever mention her will to you?"

"Never."

I wondered if tearing up the old will and writing a new one had been entirely her own idea. Or had someone suggested it? I could imagine Eunice saying, "If you want to change your will, Aunt Jo, wouldn't it be better to make one out in your own handwriting, rather than waiting for Harold Ponsby to get back?"

But again, why should Eunice have done that?

186

Joel went on, "Well, don't worry about it, darling. That lawyer will know how to straighten everything out."

I longed to tell him that there was more weighing upon my mind, much more. But how could I tell him I suspected the Andexters and Dale of such monstrous behavior when I could think of no reason for such acts?

And besides, there was the matter of proof. Even if Dale had waited until Betty Gadsen passed out one night and then injected her with a lethal dose of a muscle relaxant, and even if, later on, Eunice and probably Dale had gone to Josephine Andexter's room in the middle of the night—even if all that had happened, how could it ever be proved? Exhumation would accomplish nothing. All traces of the drug would have disappeared.

And so what did I have in the way of evidence? The presence in the Pinehaven library of a book about medical malpractice? That was no sort of evidence. A scholarly book on rare poisons might have been, but not a best seller that millions of people must have read in either hardcover or paperback, and tens of thousands must have kept as part of their personal libraries. Even if everything I suspected were true, Dale and the Andexters must have regarded the book as no sort of proof against them. Otherwise they would not have run even the remote risk that someone might open that particular book and read that particular passage. They would have destroyed the book. As it was, they hadn't bothered to get rid of it.

And so, as we drove along the dirt road through the pine forest, with the light of a three-quarter moon filtering through the trees, I tried to dismiss everything from my mind except the comfort of Joel's arm around me and the solidity of his shoulder against my cheek.

187

CHAPTER **18**

For several days I managed to keep my anxiety at bay most of the time. I even resumed work in the attic. Then on a Friday morning I walked down the path toward the lake. It was a bright day, but with a nip in the air that already hinted at the first frost.

I was about halfway down the path when I heard a cracking noise followed by a high-pitched whine. Something struck the trunk of a tree standing not two feet away from me. A piece of bark flew off, revealed the pale wood underneath.

I stood frozen for a moment and then started running toward the lake. Again a rifle's crack and the whine of a bullet. This time I did not see or hear it strike. I only knew it did not hit me. I raced on, lungs laboring, heart pounding with terror, and emerged still running onto the stone-strewn beach.

Joel caught me by the shoulders. "Darling! What is it? did those shots—"

I said, gasping for breath, "One almost hit me."

"Damn those hunters!"

"Joel, it's not the season for—"

"I know it's not. So do they. But that makes no difference to them, especially not if times are hard and they want to put free meat on their tables."

I cried, "I don't think it was someone shooting at a deer! I think he was shooting at me!"

After a moment Joel said, "Now why on earth should—"

"Please! Let's don't stand here! Let's get to the other side of the lake. Please!

"All right, darling, all right!"

He helped me into the boat, pushed it into the water. He got aboard, yanked the motor into life. We had almost reached the center of the blue, unruffled lake when he said, "Now who do you think was shooting at you?"

"Dale Carling, probably."

"Dale! Now, why—"

"Joel, please." I glanced over my shoulder toward the shore line we had left. Nothing but rocky beach and tall stand of trees. "Just listen for a while. I think they are all three in it together. They killed that wonderful old lady. And before that, Dale—it must have been Dale—killed Betty Gadsen."

"Darling, why on earth should he have—"

"Maybe because she'd become too much of a nuisance to him, or maybe because he thought that if she were still alive she might become suspicious about Josephine Andexter's death—"

While the opposite shore drew steadily closer I went on, aware that my account was pretty confused. I spoke of the book somebody had bought in a Bangor shop, and then of my unseen assailant on the subway stairs, and then of my waking up for no discernible reason the night Mrs. Andexter died, and then of the expression on Oren Wisart's face when I asked if succinylcholine had been one of the missing drugs. But jumbled as my story was, I could tell, by the increasingly appalled look in his eyes, that I was making sense to him.

I was still talking as we beached the boat and walked up to the Mustang parked beside the boathouse and got into the car.

At last he said, his face pale beneath its tan, "But for God's sake, why? Why should they do these things?"

Someone—I think it was Samuel Johnson—said that when a man knows he is to be hanged, it concentrates his mind wonderfully. Maybe being shot at has the same effect. In any event, as I was racing along that path I suddenly had thought of an answer to that question.

"It's the Conservancy. They had to get the Conservancy out of the picture."

"The what? What on earth are you talking about?"

"The Open Land Conservancy. Don't you remember? I told you about it the other night. The will she tore up left almost everything to the Conservancy. She'd had it drawn up a few years ago when she'd given up hope of Karen returning. She didn't want Eunice and Brian to have the bulk of her estate. I think she feared that they would sell the house and land for several millions to those ski resort people. Anyway, she drew up this will which left Eunice and Brian a yearly income and the rest of her estate to an organization pledged to preserve her house and land just as it was."

Joel said in a quiet voice, "I see what you mean. Their

190

problem was to get the Conservancy knocked out of her will, something they could never persuade her to do as long as she had all her faculties."

I nodded. "So they decided to make her think Karen had come back. With Dale helping, they set out to find a—a—"

"A ringer."

"Yes, that's the word. And they found me. They must have felt sure that sooner of later she would change her will back to what it had been before Karen disappeared. Once she had drawn up that holograph will, they—they killed her. And now—"

I broke off, looking out over the lake. A kingfisher dove into the blue water and then flew off with a fish flapping in its beak.

I said, "When I saw that handwritten will, I was too upset to read every word of it. But I remember that the final sentence said something like, 'If for any reason the Probate Court cannot carry out my wishes as expressed in this last will and testament, the share of my estate allotted to my granddaughter, Karen Andexter, shall in no circumstance be inherited by the Open Land Conservancy.'

"At the time I thought it was just what lawyers call an exclusionary clause. I mean, it was there to indicate that she hadn't forgotten about the Conservancy, but instead had deliberately excluded them."

I felt sure that writing that last sentence hadn't been her own idea. I could imagine Eunice saying, "Aunt Jo, that Conservancy has lots of high-powered lawyers. If you don't want them making trouble for Karen later on, you'd better make it perfectly clear that you don't want the Conservancy to inherit."

I went on, "The will didn't say anything about Eunice and Brian inheriting in case the—the granddaughter died before the will could be probated. If any of the three of them had suggested such a clause to her, she might have become suspicious. But with the granddaughter dead and the Conservancy ruled out of the picture, who would there be except Eunice and Brian to inherit all those millions in cash and real estate?"

Joel's voice was flat. "We'd better go to the police right away. Not Chief Tate. We'll drive over to Hoving Springs and see the county sheriff."

"And tell him what? That the Andexters and Dale Carling killed Josephine Andexter, and probably Betty Gadsen as well? What proof will we ever have that both of them did not die of cardiac arrest? And as for those shots a little while ago, what proof do we have that it wasn't a trigger-happy hunter?"

"All right! But we can at least tell how those three hired you to come up here and impersonate—"

"But how can we prove that their motive was anything but what I thought it was, concern for a grieving relative with only a short while to live? As for that will, they can tell the authorities just what they told me—that as soon as that lawyer returned they intended to have him straighten everything out and see to it that the bulk of her estate went to the Conservancy."

A sudden thought struck me. "Why, they can even say that I must be the one who got her to change that will in my favor."

Joel and I looked at each other. I could tell by the appalled expression in his eyes that he too was realizing how this tight-knit little community would view such a charge. On the one hand here were Eunice and Brian,

192

established members of the community and bearers of the proud name of Andexter. On the other, here was Catherine Mayhew, the classic outsider, a girl with no family behind her, a girl who'd been "some sort of actress" down in wicked New York until the Andexters, in their concern for their aged relative, had been foolish enough to hire her—

"Sure," I went on, "if we tell the authorities I'm not Karen, Eunice and Brian and Dale no longer have a motive for getting rid of me. What's more, we'll have messed up their scheme to beat the Conservancy out of all that money. But they still," I said bitterly, "will have gotten away with murder, quite literally."

He said, after a long moment, "I don't see how we can prevent them from getting away with it."

"There must be some way!" I was aware of the passion in my voice. "I'd come to love her, Joel. And she was having such—such *fun*. I think she was happier these past few weeks than anyone I've ever known. Killing her was as wicked as anything I've ever heard of. And I want them *punished!*"

"Sh-h-h!" He drew me into his arms, pressed my head against his shoulder. "You mustn't think about that now because there's no use in thinking about it. We must plan how to keep you safe—"

"If we could talk to Karen," I cut in heedlessly, "she might know something about them, something we could use to trap them."

"Darling, darling! Karen has been gone for more than eight years. How can we hope to find her?" He did not add that she was possibly, perhaps even probably, dead, but I knew he must be thinking that. "After all, detectives couldn't find her."

"Oh, yes. The detectives Eunice and Brian hired, or said they hired."

After a moment he said, "All right. Maybe they didn't really try to find her. Maybe they hoped for a long time that with Karen gone, Mrs. Andexter would make them her heirs. I still say that it's unlikely, after all this time, that we could find Karen."

I said slowly, "There's one thing that might help. Not long after she disappeared, Karen wrote her grandmother a letter. Mrs. Brill intercepted it. She told me that she had never shown it to anyone, even though she kept it. If she would show it to us—well, it might be a start toward finding Karen."

He looked out over the lake. Finally he said, "All right. We can at least talk about it."

We sat there, making plans. A few people drove up and parked behind us—a fisherman who waded out into the lake in hipboots, two teenage boys who, wearing sweaters under their life jackets, launched an orange kayak, and a gray-haired couple who walked slowly along the beach, picking up the rounded pinkish or milky white stones and dropping some of them into a brown shopping bag.

Finally Joel said in a curt voice, "Then that's how we'll do it."

He maneuvered the Mustang in the narrow road, drove past the parked cars and back into town. We stopped before the Cartwrights' white frame house. On this cool day no one sat on the front porch. Joel asked me if I wanted to come in with him, but I, feeling too raw-nerved to talk to his father, said no.

In about ten minutes Joel came out carrying a suitcase and placed it in the Mustang's trunk. He said, getting behind the wheel, "I told Dad we were going away for a few days."

"What did he say?"

"He didn't like it, of course. In his day unmarried couples didn't do things like that, at least not openly. But what else can I tell him? We'll go by the garage now. I want to leave instructions with Danny. And I want to make some phone calls."

At the garage, too, I remained in the car. Danny Cartwright, working with another man on a green station wagon, smiled and waved a wrench at me. Through the glass wall of the office I could see Joel at the telephone. He came out after a while, stood talking to his brother for a few minutes, and then returned to the Mustang.

As we drove out of the station he said, "I called a couple of airports. Not the nearest one. I was sure he wouldn't have gone there. But the one the other side of Hoving Springs and one in Langster, forty miles from here."

I waited. Joel said, "The manager at the Langster field remembered a customer who came there around ten in the morning on the same day you went to New York. One of the charter pilots flew him down to La Guardia. He hired the plane only one way, so he must have come back up here the next day by a scheduled flight."

"He was Dale?"

"Yes. He even gave his right name. The manager looked it up."

No real proof, of course. There was no law against Dale Carling going down to New York the same day that I did. But Joel and I now had no doubt as to who it was whose attack upon me had me eager to return to the

195

seeming peace and safety of Pinehaven.

We had a belated lunch at the diner. Then we drove slowly through cool mid-afternoon sunlight to Wrecker's Point and spent the rest of the day there, sometimes talking, sometimes just sitting with his arm around me and my head on his shoulder. Just after sunset we started for Pinehaven.

As Joel stopped the Mustang at the foot of the wide steps, I had a sense of eyes peering down at us through window curtains. With grim satisfaction I thought of how worried those three must be.

As soon as we walked through the door, Eunice came out of the living room into the hall, confirming my guess that she had been watching from the window. "At last! We've been so upset!"

I said, past the angry, frightened beat of the pulse in the hollow of my throat, "Upset?"

"Yes! I'd expected you back to help me with the sorting. But what was worse, we heard shots in the woods. Those dreadful hunters! They start earlier every year." With a strained smile, she said to Joel, "Forgive me for not saying hello until now, but I've been so distressed." Then to me: "Surely you must have heard the shots."

"Yes. I got out of the woods and down to the lake as fast as I could. I didn't come home this afternoon because I had the impression you were going to paint again today. Didn't you say something about it at dinner last night?"

"Perhaps I did. In fact, I started to paint, but after those shots— Anyway, quite soon Dale and Brian went into the woods looking for you. They didn't find you, of course, or any hunters either."

"Well, I'm sorry you were worried. Joel and I have just

196

been driving around. Incidentally, I've asked him for dinner. Is that all right?"

For a moment her eyes betrayed just how far from all right it was. Whatever they had planned to do or say to me this evening, obviously his presence would be an obstacle.

She smiled at Joel. "Why, of course. We'll be glad to have you."

"After dinner," I said, "we're going to start out on a trip. We'll be gone several days, if that's all right with you."

She said, after several moments, "Why, how nice! Where are you going?"

"Montreal."

"Such a charming city! Joel, wouldn't you like to pour a drink for yourself and Karen? I think you'll find almost anything you might want in the liquor cabinet in the library."

"None for me," I said, "I'm going upstairs to change."

To anyone watching from the darkness beyond the windows, I suppose the scene in the dining room that night would have seemed normal enough, five pleasant-looking people gathered around a candlelit table, serving themselves from the tureens Mrs. Brill offered. But to me the tension of those three was almost palpable. It was in the awkward movement with which Eunice almost upset her water glass. It was in the over-cordiality with which the men treated the unexpected guest, asking him about various makes of cars and about his three years at Yale. Dale even brought up the subject of the rifle fire in the woods.

"Did you happen to be close enough to hear it?"

"Oh, yes," Joel said. "I was down at the lake. Miss An-

197

dexter says you and Mr. Andexter searched the woods. Did you happen to find the rifle shells?"

Joel and I, as we sat in his car beside the boathouse, had talked of looking for the shells but decided against it. Probably, we figured, the rifleman had already recovered them and taken them from the woods. And if he hadn't, it would be dangerous for us to search along the path, with an armed man lurking somewhere among the trees.

"No," Dale said. "As a matter of fact it didn't even occur to us to keep an eye out for the shells."

A lie, of course. I was sure he had found and disposed of them. As for the rifle, he must have long since cleaned it and put it away.

A few minutes later Eunice said, "Shall we go to the library for coffee?"

"If you'll excuse me," I said, "I won't join you. I'd better go upstairs and pack."

In my room I crammed clothing into the tote. Then I added all the Catherine Mayhew identification I'd kept in the side pockets of my suitcase, and all those hundred-dollar bills, too. If our search for Karen was a prolonged one, I thought grimly, we might very well need that money.

Carrying the tote and my handbag, I went out into the silent hall. By this time Mrs. Brill would have retreated to her own quarters, leaving the Andexters and Dale and their highly unwelcome guest in the library. I moved softly along the east wing hall to its end and descended the rear stairs. On the ground floor I slipped past the partly opened door to the kitchen. I could hear Hannah and Edith's voices in there, and the rhythmic surge of the dishwasher. A few feet farther on I stopped and tapped

198

softly at Mrs. Brill's door. No response, just the sound of a TV laugh track. I knocked again, louder this time, and glanced nervously to my left. If that group in the library moved out into the hall and saw me—

The door opened. From the irritation in Mrs. Brill's face, quickly followed by surprise, I knew that she had thought it was either Hannah or Edith who had come to interrupt her well-earned leisure. "Why—"

I slipped past her into her sitting room. "Please, Mrs. Brill. Please close the door."

She did so and then moved toward the TV set. On its screen John Ritter argued with two of his female co-stars in "Three's Company." I said, "No! Please leave it on. The sound will cover our voices."

She turned a puzzled face toward me. I said, softly and swiftly, "You once mentioned a letter Karen wrote after she disappeared, a letter to her grandmother. You kept it, you told me. May I see it?" Then, as she stood motionless, still with that bewildered look, I said, "Please! I don't have much time."

For a moment more she stood there, her face unreadable now. Then without a word she turned and went into the next room. I heard a drawer slide open, then closed. She came back into the sitting room, an envelope in her hand. As if she found it unpleasant to the touch, she held it out to me by one corner.

I looked at it. It had been mailed in Scranton, Pennsylvania, a little more than eight years before. The printed return address in the lefthand corner was, surprisingly, the YWCA. I took out the single sheet of paper and unfolded it. The letter began, conventionally enough, "Dear Grandmother," but after that—

My shocked and unbelieving gaze went down the page:

199

Listen, you stupid old thing. Don't try to find me. It will do you no good. I'm sick of Muskeegan, sick of Eunice and Brian, sick of that house, and most of all I'm sick of you. You and all your sniveling, and all that more-in-sorrow-than-in-anger crap because of my getting kicked out of a stupid school I never wanted to go to in the first place.

I warn you. If you force me back there you'll *really* have trouble on your hands. I'll deal pot, not just smoke it. I'll walk naked down Main Street. I'll be the easiest lay in Muskeegan. That's right, me, Josephine Andexter's granddaughter.

Just leave me alone. Find somebody else to blubber over, and to listen to your stupid stories about people who've been dead for years.

I mean every word of this.

Karen

For me one of the most shocking things about the letter was the handwriting. One would have thought that she would have written such hate-filled words with angry slashing of her pen. Instead, the handwriting was as precise, the lines as even, as if she had been answering a wedding invitation.

How could this have been written by the same girl who, at age sixteen, had recorded that awkward but loving "poem"?

Thank God Mrs. Brill had intercepted this letter. Thank God the woman whose death I mourned had never seen it.

I laid the letter on the TV set. "You're sure it's in Karen's handwriting?" I myself was sure it was. I had seen samples of her handwriting on the backs of snapshots in the dressing table drawer in my room and in an old date book on the stand beside my bed.

"She wrote it, all right." On the TV set the two girls,

200

shrieking, chased John Ritter around a room. "But you've never seen it before, have you?"

"No."

"You're not her."

"No."

"Again and again I've had the feeling you weren't. It was hard to believe that anything, even memory loss, could change a girl that much. But I couldn't figure who else—" She broke off, and then added, "Whoever you are, thank God for you. You made her happy."

"That was the reason the Andexters gave for hiring me to come up here. They wanted me to make her happy, they said. But now— Please listen to me, Mrs. Brill. I haven't much time."

I drew a deep breath and then went on, "My name is Catherine Mayhew. When Eunice and Brian hired me, I believed it was out of love for their aunt. But, oh, Mrs. Brill! I think they killed her, in a way that no one could ever prove. You see, there's this drug that can be injected—"

For several seconds she made no sound, just stared at me from a white, rigid face. Then she said, "Why?"

"Her will. They wanted her to disinherit the Conservancy. That's why they needed to make her think her granddaughter had come back to her. Once she'd written out that new will, the one you found, they—they killed her."

Face still pale and set, she said, "But that can't be right. That will I found doesn't give the estate to them. It names you, I mean Karen—" Her face turning even whiter, she broke off. Then said, "Oh, I see."

"That's right. If I die before the will is submitted for probate, they will inherit. And today in the woods I came

201

close to dying in what would have been called a hunting accident."

I looked at her for several seconds. "Mrs. Brill, how is it that you just seem to accept the things I'm telling you?"

Her face crumpled. "Because she was getting better! Dr. Brawley said she was stronger than she had been in years. And then all of a sudden—"

Her voice was shaking now. "And I know those two. They've lived here for fifteen years. And I know that—that person they brought here. Oh, I didn't know until now they were capable of killing my poor darling. But I've known they were rotten and twisted, all three of them."

Of course. The Andexters and Dale might be able to keep everyone else ignorant about their private lives. But they couldn't keep such matters hidden from their house-keeper.

She said, still in that shaking voice, "But don't tell me there is no way of proving what they've done. Don't tell me that!"

"Maybe there is. Maybe if Joel Cartwright and I can find Karen, she'll know something we can use against them."

"But she's been gone for eight years!"

"I know. But at least we know where to start looking. That's why I wanted to see that letter."

"Tell me what I can do to help."

"Nothing. Just go on as before. Don't give them the slightest reason to suspect that you know anything. And keep that letter well hidden. We're leaving tonight. We said we were going to Montreal, which they may or may not believe. But if by any chance they find out where we're really going—"

"They won't. And I'll burn that letter right away."

I said, turning toward the door, "I must go now."

"Wait!" She went to the door, opened it, poked her head out. Then, turning to me: "All clear. But better slip up the back stairs. It's quicker."

"I know." I managed to smile. "Goodbye."

CHAPTER 19

Only minutes later I descended the main staircase. I found them all still in the library, with liqueur glasses in their hands and the Boston Pops on the TV screen. Joel, who sat on the sofa with Eunice, placed his glass on the coffee table and got to his feet. The others also stood up.

"So you're off to Montreal!" Brian said.

"Be sure to visit their underground shopping mall," Dale said. "It's really something."

I managed not to shrink back as Eunice touched my cheek with her lips.

The Mustang still stood at the foot of the steps. We got into it. "Where?" Joel asked.

"Scranton, Pennsylvania."

As we had planned that afternoon, we moved at a leisurely pace down the drive, hoping that watchers in the house would gain no impression of urgency, no hint that we were bound on anything but a pleasure trip. But once we were on the road between the tall stands of pine,

Joel speeded up. Since we had entered the house that evening, we had provided those three with no chance for a real conference. Certainly they would have one now. But it might take them only a little time to decide that they could not take the chance that we were telling the truth and that I would be back in a few days with plenty of time for them to stage another—and more successful—accident before that lawyer's return. Once they had decided that, they would of course try to keep track of us, one way or another. Even now Dale might be getting into the Porsche—

Joel asked, "Did you read the letter?"

"Yes."

"It was bad?"

"Horrible."

We did not speak again until after we had driven through the town, past the darkened garage and the high hospital gates. And even after we were on the interstate highway we said little. Joel concentrated on driving at a speed well over the legal limit. And although neither of us mentioned it, I'm sure that he as well as I was on the alert for the sudden appearance of a yellow Porsche, perhaps forcing us across the divider into oncoming traffic. A bad highway accident could be just as lethal as an accidental shooting in the woods.

We stopped for the night at a motel on the other side of the New York border. Before we reached it we had driven past three other modern, two-story motels, with plate glass window walls and with cars lined up in a parking lot. The place where we finally stopped was well off the road and much older, with neat frame cabins separated by individual garages. I understood why he had chosen it. The Mustang, driven as far as possible into the garage beside our cabin, would be less conspicuous than in a parking lot.

That far off the road, the place was very quiet. Once we'd turned off the lamp, the darkness was unbroken except for the faint glimmer from a shaded light illuminating the motel's sign. I was tired and anxious, and I know that Joel must have been too. But for a considerable while, lying embraced in the darkness, we found surcease from the thought of anything but our need for each other.

We reached Scranton around one in the afternoon the next day. Leaving the car in a public parking lot, we walked a block to the Y. A thirtyish, brown-haired woman at the desk said, "Karen Andexter? Oh, no, we don't have anyone by that name. If we did, I'd recognize it. Such a pretty name."

I said, "I didn't mean do you have anyone of that name now. I meant eight years ago."

"Eight years ago! Good heavens, I wouldn't know. I've been here only five years, and most of the other employees have been here less than that. Of course, there are old records stored down in the basement, but I—"

She broke off and then said, "Wait a minute! I think we do have someone who was here that long ago. Her name is Sally Quinn."

"Where can we find her?"

"She's in charge of the supply room on the second floor. But I'm afraid you'll have to wait down here," she said to Joel. "Men are allowed only on the ground floor."

I rode in the elevator to the second floor and walked along the bare corridor until I found a door marked "Supply Room." I knocked.

"Come in."

206

The room I walked into was little more than a cubbyhole, occupied by a brunette in her late thirties. She sat behind a metal table which held a typewriter and an open ledger. Through a doorway I could see into a larger room. Against its far wall, floor-to-ceiling shelves held stacks of sheets.

I said to the brunette, "Miss Quinn?"

She smiled. "That's right. What can I do for you?"

I suppose it was because of the pert Irish name that I had expected someone little and cute. Even though she was sitting down, I could see that she must be at least five-feet-ten, with a scrawny neck, large front teeth, and a too-long nose. Only the gray eyes were attractive, and the eager-to-please smile.

"I wanted to ask you about someone who probably stayed here a little more than eight years ago. You were here then, weren't you?"

"Oh, sure. I've been here nearly twelve years." The pleased surprise in her manner told me that she had expected me to ask for some mosquito repellant for my room, or to complain that the blankets were too short. "Pull up a chair and sit down."

The only chair available was a straight one against the cubbyhole's opposite wall. I brought it close to the desk and sat down.

"Maybe you wonder why I've been here that long," she said. "Well, the job doesn't pay much and it's not exciting, but there's a nice atmosphere for a girl alone, if you know what I mean. Now who was it you want to ask about?"

"Her name was Karen Andexter."

Her mouth dropped open. "Sure, I remember Karen, even though she was here only about a week. She was

207

terribly pretty, about eighteen and blond."

She broke off. "Why, *you* look like her. Quite a lot older, but still enough like her to be her sister. You don't mind my saying you look older, do you?"

Smiling, I shook my head.

"Silly me!" She struck her forehead with the heel of her hand. "She probably looks about the same age as you by now."

Fleetingly I reflected that Sally Quinn seemed to be someone caught in a time warp. She was like a character out of a movie back in the bad old days when it was okay to get laughs by showing a black man turn white with terror, or by portraying unmarried woman past thirty as twittering fools.

"You certainly do look like her. A cousin, maybe?"

"No. I'm trying to trace her for legal reasons."

Sally looked worried. "I wouldn't want to cause her any trouble."

"You won't. It's because of a legacy that we're trying to locate her." That, I reflected wryly, was at least part of the truth. "My boss—he's a lawyer—is handling the estate."

She looked both reassured and pleasantly excited. "Whose estate? Her grandmother's? The one she ran away from?" I must have looked startled because she said, "You know she ran away, don't you?"

"Yes, we know. Do you mind telling me how you know?"

"She told me about it after she'd been here three or four days. She seemed nice, not stuck on herself the way a girl that pretty might be, and so we got to be friends. That night we were talking in my room—I had a room here then, just the way I do now—and she seemed—" She broke off. "Say, are you sure you're not related?"

"I'm sure."

"Then I guess it's okay to tell you she seemed sort of high, like she'd been smoking grass up on the roof. That happens sometimes. Anyway, she told me she'd run away from some little town up in Maine. I'd already guessed she'd been in some sort of trouble, someplace. I mean, she had such a wild, nervous look about her."

I leaned forward. "Did she say why she ran away?"

"No, but when I said her family might be looking for her, she said nobody gave a damn about her except her grandmother, and even her grandmother wouldn't want to look for her, once she'd read the letter she'd mailed to her."

"Letter?"

"I'd seen her writing a letter down in the lobby, on Y stationery. Maybe she didn't have enough money to afford letter paper of her own."

"Did she tell you what was in the letter?"

"No. And when I asked her that, she began to cry. Then she turned sort of nasty and told me to mind my own business. And then she got up and left my room. She apologized the next day." Sally's voice turned wistful. "But from then on we weren't really friends."

"Do you know where she went after she left here?"

My pulses leaped when she nodded. "She and this other girl went to Cleveland. The other girl's name was Bitsy Something-or-other. I don't remember her last name, but that crazy first name stuck in my mind. She said it was her legal name—Bitsy plus whatever the last name was. She'd gone to court to have it changed from Ethel Something-or-other.

"She wasn't the sort of girl who usually stays at a Y."

209

There was disapproval in Sally's voice. "I guess she came here because she was between jobs and sort of hard up. She was a dancer. Not ballet. Nightclubs, that sort of thing. She was older than Karen, maybe twenty-four, twenty-five. I hated to see a kid like Karen getting mixed up with her."

Was Sally resentful over Karen's rejecting her friendship for Bitsy's? Probably. But I sensed that she also had been genuinely concerned about the strange young runaway.

"And so Karen went with her to Cleveland?"

"Yes. Bitsy had been promised a job in a floor show there, and she said she could get Karen a job too, if only as a hatcheck girl."

"Do you remember the name of the nightclub?"

"Sure! Karen sent me a postcard when she'd been there about six months. Wait a sec. I'll get it."

Her room must have been on that floor because she returned, if not in a second, in less than two minutes. The postcard, the sort hotels and restaurants give away to their customers, bore the photograph of a room filled with small tables, all empty. There was a bandstand, also empty, and a dance floor. In white type across the lower part of the picture were the words "Club Jacko, where Cleveland stays up late." Printed in the same type were an address and phone number.

I turned the card over. In a handwriting already familiar to me, Karen had written, "Hiya, Sal! Guess what? I'm in the floor show now. If you ever get to Cleveland, come see me. Love, Karen."

I said hopefully, "But you got other cards and letters from her, didn't you?"

"No. I wrote to her at that club several times, but she

210

never answered. Too busy, I guess."

But she'd still kept the card Karen had written to her all those years ago. I handed it back to her. "Thank you, Miss Quinn. You've been very helpful."

That night, in our darkened room in a motel on the other side of the Ohio state line, I asked on sudden impulse, "Do you still feel you loved Karen?"

"Sure I loved her. Oh, it wasn't what I feel for you. It was love-at-twenty, hell and heaven, pain and passion all mixed up. Even when she took up with Danny I still loved her, and I went on feeling that way for about a year after she ran away without even giving me a phone call first. Finally the love died. Maybe the bitterness would have too, if I hadn't been aware of Danny down there in that Florida prison."

"But you don't feel bitter toward her now, do you?"

"No. Loving you has ended that. What I feel now has shown me how immature I was then. And Danny and Karen were of course even younger, a pair of kids playing with drugs instead of matches."

He fell silent, hands locked behind his head, gaze fixed on the dimly visible ceiling. This was one of the big chain motels, all plate glass and chrome and big-screen TV in the rooms, and, in the lobby, imitation rubber plants and fake brick walls. When, following the direction on the motel's highway sign, he had turned off toward this place, I had said, "I think you'll have to leave the car in full view there," and he had answered, "I've decided it won't matter."

Now, in this room illuminated only by light from the parking lot filtering through the drawn draperies, it was hard to make out Joel's expression. I sensed rather than

211

saw that he looked worried.

I said, "Why is it you decided that leaving the car in full view wouldn't matter?"

He was silent for at least half a minute and then said, "I think someone already has spotted us and is on our trail."

I grew rigid. "Dale Carling?"

"No, and neither of the Andexters. But he must be someone—probably a detective—they phoned soon after we left. I haven't got a good look at him—he keeps a hat pulled well down—but he's a beefy guy, around fifty, I'd say."

He paused and then went on, "You remember that parking lot where we left the car while we were in the Y?"

"Of course."

"When we drove away I noticed that a blue Buick with Pennsylvania plates had followed us out of the lot. I didn't think anything of it until later on. When we came out of that place where we'd stopped for a hamburger, I saw the same car and driver parked outside. I don't know when he followed us back onto the highway, but twice in the late afternoon I saw him, several cars back."

"But, Joel! Couldn't it have been just coincidence? If the Andexters phoned him after we left, they'd have had to talk it over first. We must have gotten a good head start. And so how could he have found us so soon?"

"Because the Andexters had told him where he could find us."

"But how on earth—"

"They must have figured out what we were up to —looking for Karen, I mean. And I'm convinced now that they must have sent detectives over her trail long ago. Oh, sure. They told their aunt that they hadn't been able to trace her beyond Augusta, Maine. The last thing they wanted to do was to restore her to her grandmother. In those days they must have hoped that if Karen was missing long enough, they themselves would replace her in the old lady's affections."

"And in her will. They couldn't have had any idea back then that she would take it into her head to leave everything to the Conservancy."

"Exactly. But to get back to the detectives they hired eight years ago. They surely must have picked up her trail. It must have been duck soup, finding bus drivers and ticket sellers and so on who remembered a pretty, up-set-looking eighteen-year-old. They followed her trail to the Scranton Y. That's why that beefy character showed up there today."

"You mean, you think he's one of the detectives they hired eight years ago?"

"Maybe. But even if he's someone entirely different, the Andexters would have been able to tell him he might find us there. I'll bet he already knows that our next stop is Cleveland."

I tried to fight down my alarm. What if they had set a man to trailing us? That was all he would do—watch us and report back. If he was some thug they had hired to harm us, surely he would have done so by now. He could have shot us down three hours ago. It was about then that we had emerged after dinner from a restaurant well off the highway and walked through the darkness to our car.

Joel said abruptly, "I think we ought to give this up. I think we should go to the police."

"No! We've been all over that. If we'd had any evidence, we could have gone to the sheriff in Hoving

213

Springs. But we didn't have any evidence then, and what additional evidence do we have now? Just that you *think* a man in a blue Buick has been following us."

"All right. Maybe there's no use in going to the police. But if I could hide you someplace, keep you safe—"

"Darling, I won't be safe until those three are behind bars for killing my—for killing Josephine Andexter and for trying to kill me. And our only hope of proving what they've done is that Karen knows something, something we can use against them."

"But if you could hide away someplace while I go on looking for Karen—"

"No! I'd be terrified. I'll feel safer, far safer, if I'm with you."

"All right," he said, after a long moment, "we'll go on." He drew me close. "But let's just forget about it for a little while."

CHAPTER **20**

THE NEXT MORNING we traveled across Ohio along a wide highway so smooth, and through green countryside so pleasant but monotonous, that I thought of how much more exciting transcontinental travel must have been during the early days of the automobile, when narrow dirt roads led you through little towns, and past farmyards, and over wooden bridges.

We both kept an eye out for the blue Buick with the burly man at the wheel, but we didn't see him. I began to hope, and I'm sure Joel did too, that his seeing the same car and driver several times the day before had been a matter of coincidence.

In Cleveland we found the nightclub without difficulty. At least from the outside, it was not the glamorous place one might have expected from that postcard. Located in a shabbier section of the business district, it occupied the ground floor of a three-story red brick building. The two plate glass windows, except for

215

twin circles left clear, were coated with blue paint. Above the double swing doors an unlighted neon sign said "Jocko's."

We tried the doors. They didn't yield. Joel knocked, and after a few moments we heard someone withdrawing the bar. A black man, holding a long-handled push broom, opened one of the doors and looked out at us. Joel said, "May we see the manager?"

"This way."

We followed him across a vestibule into the main room. Here daylight coming through the circles of clear glass was augmented by a big drop light. It glared down on the bare tables covered with upended chairs, and showed chipped places on the murals of Paris scenes—the Eiffel Tower and caped gendarmes and mademoiselles in impossibly high heels and little else—that covered the walls.

The janitor stopped at a door marked "Samuel Dewhurst, Manager" and knocked. A voice called, "Come in."

The black man opened the door and said, "People to see you."

"Well, send them in, send them in." Then, rising from behind a littered desk, "Have a seat, folks, and tell me what I can do for you."

He didn't look like my idea of a night club manager. He was about sixty, with a mostly bald head and with brown eyes that were both friendly and sad, like a basset hound's.

We sat down in straight chairs near his desk. Joel said, "My name is Cartwright, and this is Miss Mayhew. We're trying to locate two girls who were in the floor show here seven or eight years ago."

"Before my time," Mr. Dewhurst said. "A fellow named Barney Clay owned the place back then. Another fellow bought it, and then I bought it from him." From the look he threw around the little office, I gathered he was asking himself why.

"But Barney Clay is still in Cleveland. Runs a cut-rate ticket agency. If you give me the names of the girls, I could phone him up right now and ask him."

"We'd certainly appreciate that," Joel said, and I said, "One of the girls was named Karen Andexter—"

"That spelled with a K?" He had pulled a notepad toward him.

"Yes. Karen Andexter. We don't know the last name of the other girl, but her first name was Bitsy."

He wrote on the pad for a moment and then picked up the phone and dialed. Evidently Barney Clay employed no assistant, because Mr. Dewhurst said, almost immediately, "Hi, Barney. Say, I got a couple of folks here who are looking for two girls who used to work here at the club. One was named Bitsy. These folks don't know her last name. The other was Andexter. First name Karen, with a K."

He kept saying, "I see, I see," and writing on the pad. Then he said, "Thanks, Barn. See you," and hung up.

"Barney remembers both girls," he told us, "but has no idea where Karen is now. Bitsy is still here in Cleveland, though. She's married to a guy named Halloran. You want the address?"

"We'd appreciate it."

Mr. Dewhurst ripped the top sheet off the pad and handed it to Joel. "That address is on the other side of town. You folks got a street map?"

Joel shook his head. Mr. Dewhurst reached into a

217

lower drawer of his desk and brought out a folded map. "Take this with you."

Joel said, "Don't you need that?"

"I got a drawerful of them. Until it went broke, I used to run a gas station."

"Well, thank you very much," Joel said, and I added, "We certainly appreciate it."

"Pleasure," Mr. Dewhurst said.

It wasn't until we were out on the sidewalk that I realized that he had never asked why we were trying to find two girls who had worked at Jocko's years ago.

The Halloran house was a small green frame bungalow on a street of similar houses, many with pickup trucks parked in their driveways. A tricycle stood on the walk and an overturned toy fire engine lay on the lawn.

Joel rang the bell. The door opened, revealing a somewhat overweight brunette of thirty-odd standing behind the screen. Beside her, bowlegged and solemn-faced, stood a toddler in a pink romper.

I said, "Mrs. Halloran?" Joel and I had decided that since we would be dealing with a woman I had better start the conversation.

"Yes."

"My name is Catherine Mayhew, and this is Joel Cartwright. We're trying to find a girl named Karen An-dexter, and we thought you might be able to help us."

She looked from one to the other of us and then unhooked the screen door. "All right. Come in."

We stepped into a living room with a brown wall-to-wall carpet thickly strewn with toys. Mrs. Halloran lifted the toddler, unprotesting, into a playpen in one corner of the room. Through an archway I could see into a dining room where two boys of perhaps four and three, making

218

buzz-buzz noises, maneuvered toy racing cars over a floor equally cluttered with toys. Although the Halloran house was modest, the Halloran offspring, apparently, were well-endowed with generous aunts and uncles and grand-parents.

Bitsy Halloran was less trusting than Mr. Dewhurst, or perhaps just more curious. As soon as we were seated, she in a maple armchair, we on a worn green sofa, which already held a toy filling station and a stuffed green frog, she asked, "How is it you're looking for Karen?"

I said, "It's in connection with a legacy. Mr. Cart-wright and I work for a law firm that is handling the matter."

"Her grandmother died?"

"Yes."

"And she left Karen money?"

"Yes."

Bitsy looked surprised. After a moment she asked, "How is it you came here?"

I explained about Sally Quinn and Mr. Dewhurst. Bitsy said that she remembered someone like Sally "vaguely." I thought of how little this harried-looking mother of three resembled the girl—"not the sort who usually stays at the Y"—of Sally Quinn's recollection.

Bitsy's dark eyes were studying me. "You're a relative of Karen's, aren't you?"

I shook my head. "I know I look a lot like her. People have told me so. But we're not related." I paused. "Do you know where Karen is now?"

"Last I heard, she was in Chicago. As I guess you know, I got her this job in the floor show at Jocko's. She couldn't sing much or dance either, but she was so pretty it didn't matter. Then five years ago this fellow from

Chicago came to the club. Karen fell for him. He told her that he was married but getting a divorce—*that* old line—and wanted to take her back to Chicago with him.

"I warned her that the guy was just a small-time hood. So did Barney. Barney Clay owned Jocko's back then, and he'd known this Chicago fellow for years. But she wouldn't listen."

Joel asked, "What was the Chicago man's name?"

"Farrow. Charlie Farrow."

"Is Karen still with him?"

"I have no idea. She never wrote to me after she left. I guess she stayed sore over the things I'd said about Charlie Farrow. I got married a few months after she left, and since then I've been so busy I'd pretty well forgotten about her."

I asked, "Do you know if Charlie Farrow is still in Chicago?"

"I imagine he is. I gathered he was well-established there, if you can use that expression about people like him. He runs something called Farrow Enterprises, or at least did. It's supposed to have something to do with boxing, but Barney said his main interests were in gambling and dope, in a nickel-and-dime sort of way, of course."

I said, "You seemed surprised when I told you that Karen's grandmother had left her money."

"I certainly was surprised. Karen told me that she had fixed it so that her grandmother would never have anything more to do with her."

"Fixed it?"

"She wrote the old lady a terrible letter. She told me some of the things in it, and they certainly were terrible."

"But why? Why did she do it?"

After a long moment Bitsy answered, "She thought she was going insane. She told me so, back there in the Scranton Y. There was insanity in her family, you know. And there were these cousins of hers living with her and her grandmother. Not first cousins. They were years older than her, the niece and nephew of her grandmother. Karen got the idea that they wanted to get rid of her, one way or another, and that having her declared insane would be one way of doing it."

"Did she say why she thought they'd want to do that?"

"Because then the old lady almost certainly would name them as Karen's legal guardians. That way they would have control of the estate after the grandmother died, even if her will made Karen her heir."

"But I still don't understand," I said. "What reason did she have to think that there was anything wrong with her mind? I've heard that she had—difficulties, been expelled from a private school and so on. But surely that wasn't reason enough to think that she might be certifiably insane."

"She'd begun to hear voices," Bitsy said. "At night in her room. People calling her name and saying crazy things. They'd say, 'Karen, we know you. Karen, you're one of us.' "

Bitsy's voice had become soft and high and thin. I knew that she must be imitating young Karen's voice as she told her story there in the Scranton Y. "Just hearing her tell about it made chills run down my back."

Chills were running down my own spine now. I recalled the sounds I had heard my first night at Pinehaven. That thin, mournful sound, sometimes a whisper, sometimes rising to a wail.

The keening of wind, I had decided, and undoubtedly

221

that was right because after Brian Andexter replaced the cap on the vent outlet, there had been no more such sounds.

Right after Karen left—right after they had sent that frightened teenager fleeing from her home—they must have recapped that old vent. Sometime during the subsequent years it must have become loosened and then fallen off. I wondered for how long the wind had made a soft wailing in the empty room before I came there to hear it.

"It wasn't just that she was afraid of what her cousins might do to her," Bitsy said. "She didn't want her grandmother to see her locked up in an asylum. She thought a lot of her grandmother, Karen did. I told her her grandmother would probably be less unhappy over her being locked up, if that ever happened to her, than over her running away and then writing a cruel letter. But she couldn't see it that way."

When we finally found Karen, it would be good to be able to tell her that her grandmother had never seen the letter.

Bitsy said, "It's nice that Karen's come into money. But I hope that when you find her she isn't still with that Charlie Farrow. He'd just take it away from her." She looked at Joel. "If you want to use our phone to call Chicago information, there it is, right beside you. You could ask them if they've got a listing for Farrow Enterprises."

"Thank you."

From the table at his end of the couch Joel took the phone book and opened it, evidently to get the number of Chicago information. He replaced the book, lifted the phone from its cradle, dialed. In the dining room one of

222

the small boys began to howl. Bitsy cried, "Joey! If you hit Paulie one more time, I promise you—"

The howling subsided to a whimper. Joel hung up the phone. "There's a listing for Farrow Enterprises, all right." He took a bill from his wallet and placed it under the phone. "That's for the call."

"Thank you. I'd like to have said 'Be my guest,' but money's sort of tight these days."

"You've helped a lot," I said, "and we're more than grateful."

"When you find Karen, be sure to tell her I've got three boys. And ask her to write to me."

Joel and I said goodbye to her and then went down the walk, past the tricycle and the overturned fire truck.

Just before we got into the Mustang I looked to my left and saw, parked perhaps a hundred yards away at the curb, a dark blue Buick with a heavyset man at the wheel.

Although Joel said nothing about it at the moment, just got behind the wheel and drove to the corner and turned right, I knew that he also had seen the man.

CHAPTER 21

I F HE FOLLOWED us onto the interstate highway we did not see him, not once during the rest of that day. And the next morning, after we had checked out of our motel about twenty miles from Chicago, we still did not see the dark Buick. But then, as Joel pointed out, he could have switched cars.

The office of Farrow Enterprises was in a Loop district building that looked both fairly new and cheaply constructed, its lobby narrow and floored with some sort of fake marble, its small elevator shaking slightly as it ascended. The secretary in Farrow's outer office was middle-aged and plain. We had expected his secretary, if he had one, to ask why we wanted to see her boss. But all she asked was our names.

She went into the inner office, came out almost immediately. "Mr. Farrow will see you."

Farrow's office was only a little larger than his secretary's. Its knotty pine walls were covered with photographs of boxers in loose trunks, gloved hands poised menacingly. He got up from behind his desk as we entered and shook our hands. I'd seen the startled look in his eyes at first sight of me, but all he said was, "Have a seat and tell me what's on your minds."

Mr. Dewhurst had not looked like my idea of a nightclub owner, but Charlie Farrow came near to my preconceived notion of what Bitsy had called a hood. Oh, not that he was swarthy, or bore visible scars. But the lids over his brown eyes seemed at permanent half-mast, and his voice had a rasping quality. Fleetingly I wondered about that rasp. Was it the result of too much booze and too many smuggled-in-from-Havana cigars? Or did men on the fringes of organized crime talk that way in imitation of the big shots, the ones who testified before Senatorial investigating committees? He was good-looking, though, in a macho and vaguely sinister sort of way, with thick dark hair and regular although rather heavy features. I could see how he might have attracted a self-destructive girl not long out of her teens.

Joel said, "We're trying to trace a girl named Karen Andexter."

Instead of answering Joel, Farrow shifted his gaze to me. "What relation are you to her?"

"None."

"Don't hand me that."

"It's true. I know I look like her, but we're not related. They say everyone has at least one double someplace. I guess I'm hers."

There was disbelief in the hooded eyes, but he didn't pursue the matter. Instead he turned to Joel. "What do you want with Karen?"

"It's about a legacy left to her. We work for the law

firm that is handling the estate."

"Her grandmother's estate?"

"Yes."

"A big one?"

Joel nodded.

"She used to tell me she had a rich grandmother, but I thought she was just making it up."

He broke off. I could almost see him wondering if he could reap any advantage from the situation. Evidently he decided in the negative because he said, with a shrug in his voice: "What the hell. Water under the bridge." Then: "How did you know I knew Karen?"

"Because we talked with a girl who worked with Karen at a Cleveland night club," Joel said. "Her name is Bitsy—Bitsy Halloran, now. She told us Karen had gone to Chicago with you."

He smiled. "I remember Bitsy. She didn't like me. Sure, I brought Karen to Chicago. I rented her a nice little apartment fairly near the lake, and everything was just fine for a couple of years. Then she started really using. Not just pot, but anything else she could get her hands on. I got no use for a girl after she's gotten into dope. I gave her a thousand dollars and told her to get lost."

Silence settled down. I could see that Farrow's words had made Joel incapable of speech for the moment, and so I was the one who asked, "Do you have any idea where she is now?"

"As a matter of fact, I do. Or at least I know where she was six months ago. A friend of mine who'd just got back from Vegas said that he'd seen her at the Rancho Mesquite."

"The what?"

After a moment he said, "You mean you never heard of it, lady? Why, it's famous. I don't know how to explain in a polite way. Well, maybe I do. It's a house run by a madam. Places like that are legal in Nevada."

I was silent for several seconds and then asked, "Where is it, exactly?"

"Out in the desert, twenty miles or so from Vegas."

We left after that. We thanked him before we walked out the door, or at least I did.

As we descended in the shaky little elevator I looked at Joel's set face. On impulse I cried, "If it's going to be so painful for you—I mean, *I* could go out there—"

"Don't talk nonsense. I'd never let you go on by yourself. Besides, I think I knew from the first that if we ever found her, it would be in some such place as that."

We saw no sign of the blue Buick as Joel maneuvered the Mustang through city traffic and then out onto the interstate highway. About thirty miles west of Chicago we stopped for lunch at a chain restaurant. As we sat in a booth eating grilled bacon and tomato sandwiches, Joel asked, "Would you mind driving until quite late tonight?"

"Of course not. But why?"

"To find out whether or not anyone is still following us."

We drove on across the gentle green landscape. For nearly two hours I took the wheel. When we stopped around seven at a motel, one of a large chain, Joel made a reservation for a room, not at that motel, but at one fifty miles ahead. Then we went into the dining room. Because we were both tired from the day's driving and from that interview with Farrow, we took our time over dinner. When we emerged from the diner we saw that

227

the moon was up. Only a little past full, it flooded the earth with blue-white radiance. We rejoined the steady parade of cars. Around eleven Joel turned onto an exit ramp.

We passed two hamburger places, both still open, and then drove along a stretch of county highway hideous with discount houses and shopping malls, all closed for the night. Back on the interstate, traffic had become thin. Here it was almost nonexistent. We drove through a small town where every business establishment was dark except for one bar. Then we were out in open country. Here there was no traffic at all. We drove for about three miles along a two-lane road that led past open fields and stretches of woodland. We met no cars, and no headlights shone in our rearview mirror. Finally Joel stopped at the roadside. No light except moonlight. No sound except the shrilling of katydids, probably from the oak in the cow pasture at our left, and the distant barking of some farm dog.

"So we're not being followed now. I guess we lost him."

"Maybe. Or maybe they've called him off."

"But why would they?"

"Because they must have kept track of her all these years. And so after we called on Farrow in Chicago, they must know where we are headed now. There's no longer any need to have us followed."

He made a U-turn in the moon-flooded road. We drove back to the interstate.

CHAPTER **22**

THE MUSTANG carried us westward. The green fields and
placid streams of Illinois and Iowa gave way to flatter
and drier Kansas, its golden stands of wheat waiting for
harvest. My hometown of Prairie Center was a couple of
hundred miles away, in the southeastern part of the state,
but until well after we crossed the Colorado border
memories of that little town and of my mother crowded
out everything else, even the thoughts of our perhaps
perilous destination. We crossed the Rockies and descended into the sort of country neither of us had ever
seen before, the dry canyons and cedar-dotted mesas and
fantastic rock formations of Utah, and then the desert of
southern Nevada, all sand and mesquite and grotesque
cactus plants.

Out of the flatness the soaring towers of Las Vegas rose
like a mirage. Even when we were in the town it seemed
unreal, like some vast carnival that might vanish without
a trace.

It was midafternoon when we drove through, and the huge neon signs advertising hotels stood unlighted against the intensely blue sky. Nevertheless, the casinos and bars were all open. Men and women with taut faces, many carrying paper cups, moved in and out of the casinos. Those cups puzzled us until we realized they must be filled with coins. Having won—or lost—playing one establishment's slot machines, people moved along the street to try their luck at another. I had heard that Las Vegas never slept, that twenty-four hours a day the slot machines jangled and the dice rattled and the gamblers, many of whom would leave the city broke, refueled their energies at the ever-open bars. I could well believe it. There was something both keyed up and weary in the atmosphere.

Back there someplace, at some motel or gas station, Joel must have learned the exact directions to Rancho Mesquite because on the far side of town he turned unhesitatingly onto a narrower but well-paved road. Signs frequently blocked our view of the desert landscape, signs advertising hotels, and casinos, and marriage chapels. "You Furnish the Bride, We Furnish Everything Else."

And then the signs for Rancho Mesquite began to appear. Comparatively small signs that said "Rancho Mesquite, 18 miles." And then fifteen miles. And then ten. Neat, respectable-looking signs, as if trafficking in women's bodies was just another business, like selling Wall Street securities, or groceries, or garden rakes. Beneath my anxiety I felt a stir of anger, but whether its main focus was men, or human nature, or even the Omnipotent, I could not have said.

Another neat sign. "Rancho Mesquite. Take next road left."

The road onto which we turned was a dirt one but well kept up. If the last rare rainfall in this arid region had carved gullies, they had all been filled in. No roadside signs obscured the view over flats barren of everything except cacti and clumps of mesquite. And the only other vehicle we saw was a small green camper parked out on the hard-baked sand.

Very soon we could see a building ahead. As we drew closer it took shape as a sprawling, two-story, ranch-style house. With its red tiled roof, white stucco facade, and long second-story balcony, it was startlingly like the house in a once-popular TV series about a western family. Over the broad front door was a yoke for oxen. Massive and worn-looking, it might well have once been the property of some family struggling across the plains and deserts toward California.

To the left of the house was a parking lot, totally empty. Perhaps Rancho Mesquite was closed to customers at this hour. We parked the car. Pulse rapid, I walked with Joel to the front door. He pushed a button. From somewhere inside the house came the muted sound of chimes.

At least a full minute passed before the door opened, revealing a plump Mexican woman of about forty. Although undoubtedly a domestic, she did not wear any sort of traditional uniform. Her hair, in two black braids, hung over the shoulders of her white cotton blouse. Her full red skirt, printed with yellow flowers, reached nearly to her sandaled feet.

Her welcoming smile turned to surprise as she realized that not only a man but a woman stood on the doorstep. Then, as her gaze concentrated upon me, I saw terrified shock in her face. With a smothered scream, she backed

231

away from the door.

The sunlight was so bright that I could see only a little way into the shadowy room beyond the doorway. But I heard another door open someplace, and a woman's voice say, "Juana! What is it?" The reply was a rapid stream of Spanish. The other woman said something also in Spanish, and then added, in English, "Get back to your work. I'll see to this."

I heard the sound of drapery rings rattled along a rod. The room brightened somewhat. Then she was standing before us, a tall brunette of about fifty. Handsome and full-figured, she appeared the sort of woman who is appointed chairman of the opera board—until you looked into her eyes. They were brown and slightly prominent and utterly cold.

Her gaze moved from Joel to me and then back again. "Yes?"

Joel said, "We're looking for a girl named Karen Andexter."

"Was that her right name? We knew her as Karen Jones." Her gaze moved back to me. "How are you related to her?"

"I'm not." How many times, I wondered, had I been asked that question in one form or another? "I know I resemble her closely, but we're not related."

"You certainly do resemble her, so much so that Juana thought you were Karen." She paused. "What is this all about?"

"A legacy that has been left to Karen."

After a moment she stepped aside. "Very well. Come in."

The draperies at all but one of the wide windows were closed. Still, there was enough light for me to get an

232

overall impression of the big room we entered. It might have been the lounge of a handsome ski resort. A wide-boarded floor of lustrous dark wood, scattered with Navajo rugs. Luxurious leather sofas and armchairs. A piano. A small mahogany bar with four red leather stools. Along the lefthand wall a handsome staircase, its steps of the same dark wood as the floor, led upward.

Only a large oil painting behind the bar, showing a woman in high-heeled red shoes and nothing else, indicated the nature of the establishment.

She opened a door into a small office. In contrast to the room we had crossed, this one was almost spartan, furnished with a rolltop desk, now open, a swivel chair, and two straight ones. She sat down in the swivel chair and waved us to the other two.

"Karen is dead."

It came as no shock. I'd known it ever since the maid retreated from me, terror in her face. I looked at Joel. His expression was wooden. "When?"

"About three months ago. It was food poisoning."

After a moment he asked, "Did any of the other— Did anyone else get it?"

"No, but that's what it was. The doctor said so and put it on her death certificate. We think she may have eaten some shrimp that the cook had left in the refrigerator too long. Karen was trying to lose weight, but she was undisciplined about it, as she was about everything, and so she'd starve herself at meals and then sneak into the kitchen for food binges."

I said, "Could something else have caused it? I mean, could it have been food she got in some restaurant?"

"It's not likely. Some man had called her and asked her to meet him in town for dinner, but that was two or three days before she got sick."

I said, before I thought, "You allow that? Meeting men on the outside?"

"Of course I allow it." The cold animosity in her face made me almost feel that she had guessed the thoughts I'd had when I saw the Rancho Mesquite roadside signs. "This is a legitimate business establishment, not a prison."

Despite her hostility, I persisted, "Do you know who the man was?"

"No. Another of my girls saw Karen with him in a restaurant, though. She said he was dark and good-looking and reminded her of some old-time movie actor, I forget which one."

I was sure I knew which one. And yet it couldn't have been Dale who poisoned her, at least not the night he'd taken her to dinner.

Joel asked, "Where is Karen buried?"

For the first time the woman sounded a little disconcerted. "In a municipal cemetery not far from here."

Municipal cemetery. Potter's field.

She went on, "I couldn't be expected to stand the expense of a private burial. Even as it was, she died owing me money."

Neither Joel nor I commented on that. Instead he asked, "Where is this cemetery?"

"It's about ten miles from here. Just go back to the main road and turn right for a couple of miles. A few yards after you pass a boarded-up hamburger stand you'll come to another road branching off to the right. Follow that for about eight miles and you'll be at the cemetery."

She stopped speaking and then asked, "Was it much money?"

234

"Her legacy?" Joel said. "Yes, it's a lot of money."

"Well, too bad she missed out on it. Once she told one of the other girls that she had a rich grandmother, but none of us believed that." She paused. "Where was she from?"

"Maine," Joel said.

"She told us New Hampshire."

We left after that. She remained seated in her swivel chair. As we crossed the big room toward the front door, I saw movement to my right and turned my head. Three young women, curious to see the visitor whom Juana had thought to be a ghost, had gathered on the staircase.

Neither of us spoke until we had almost reached the main road. Then I said, "I'm sorry, Joel."

He didn't answer, but just let go of the wheel long enough to squeeze my hand. When we reached the main road he turned right.

I said, "So Dale Carling couldn't have poisoned her."

"Oh, yes, he could have."

"But Joel! How? If she didn't come down with food poisoning until forty-eight hours or more after he took her to dinner—"

"I'll tell you how. Once I had to get rid of some rats at the garage. The pharmacist who sold me rat poison told me that any phosphorus-based poison may take two to three days to work, although sometimes it takes effect within a few hours. Then he said, 'And it acts the same way with people.'

"Carling must have hoped the reaction would be delayed," he went on, "and he did luck out. But he'd probably have gotten away with it even if the symptoms had shown up only a few hours later. They're the same as food poisoning—vomiting, diarrhea, cramps, and so on."

His voice became bitter. "And anyway, how much trouble would a doctor like that take with a diagnosis, a whorehouse doctor probably too drunken or incompetent to get other patients?"

For perhaps a minute we drove in silence. Then I said, "I suppose he felt he couldn't use the muscle-relaxant drug again, even if he had some left."

"No. Karen wasn't a fragile old lady or a middle-aged alcoholic. Oh, I'm sure she'd gone on using drugs, including booze, but he couldn't have counted on her getting passing-out drunk, the way he could with Betty Gadsen."

After a moment I said, "He must have killed her soon after I answered that ad in the *Village Voice*. Dale wasn't around all the time while I was practicing my Maine accent and having my hair lightened and so on. He must have flown out to Las Vegas, fed her that poison, whatever it was, and then flown back to New York."

"Yes. Even after eight years, they couldn't be sure but what the real Karen would come home, and that would have blown their plans sky high."

He paused and then added, "Well, we'll find out what poison he used to kill Karen."

"Exhumation?"

He nodded. "We'll get a court order. And we'll summon that girl at Rancho Mesquite, whoever she is, to identify Carling as the man she saw with Karen in a Las Vegas restaurant."

We passed the abandoned hamburger stand. It must have been closed for some time because the boards nailed across it had taken on that gray-satin sheen of wood long exposed to the sun. A few yards farther on we again turned right. This was not like the well-kept road that led

236

to Rancho Mesquite, but narrow and rutted and pot-holed. We met no cars and saw only one building. From a crossbarred gate, a road that was little more than a track led past a horse-filled corral to a house and a tall wind-mill set in a grove of cottonwoods. Nailed to the gate was a weathered sign that read, "X Bar K Ranch. Saddle horses for hire."

We continued on down the road through the brilliant afternoon sunlight. And there it was, the pitiful little cemetery. A low fence of baling wire strung between sun-bleached posts surrounded it on three sides. On the fourth side the sandy earth dropped away into a gully. There was a crossbar gate in the fence, wide enough for a car to drive through. We did not drive in but left the Mustang standing outside the fence.

We walked down between two rows of the mounded graves. Most were unmarked, but here and there a wooden cross stood erect, or leaned to one side, or, in one case, had toppled onto the mound. Without saying anything we walked to the newest-looking grave, near the edge of the waist-deep gully. This one had an actual headstone, although a very inexpensive-looking one, a thin slab of marble engraved with the words "Karen Jones." Just that. No dates. I felt sure that, cheap as it was, the proprietor of Rancho Mesquite had not bought it. The girls there must have chipped in for it.

Only a faint wind disturbed the stillness. Standing beside Joel, I continued to look at the headstone that marked the end of Karen Andexter's short and stormy passage through life. I thought of those snapshots of her and her poem to her grandmother. I thought of the fear—the terrible fear of a madhouse—that had sent her fleeing along a path that led eventually to Rancho

237

Mesquite. And I could find only one thing to be glad about. I was glad that Josephine Andexter had never known what eventually happened to the little girl she had held on her lap in one of those snapshots.

The sound of a car's engine. A green camper was approaching, surely the same one we had seen parked a few yards to the side of the road leading to Rancho Mesquite. Top-heavy, it swayed slightly over the rough surface.

It turned into the cemetary gate. Its door opened and a man got out, dapper in suede jacket and chinos, dark hair shining in the sunlight. He reached back into the vehicle's front seat. His appearance here was so sudden and unexpected that I don't think I realized he was Dale Carling until he drew the rifle out. He brought it to his shoulder and fired the first shot. Almost simultaneously I heard the rifle's crack and the bullet's hornetlike singing.

Joel's arm swung hard against me, knocking me backward into the gully. Half-stunned, I lay for several seconds on the gully's pebble-strewn bed. Another shot sounded, and another. I rolled over onto my hands and knees, got to my feet. I saw Joel crouched low, dodging among the sandy mounds, the weathered crosses. Perhaps it was because Dale faced west, with the lowering sun in his eyes, that he had trouble hitting his target.

Joel leaped the baling wire fence, wrenched the Mustang's door open, got inside. He must have switched on the engine with one hand and hit the window button with the other because I heard the engine's roar and saw the glass rise almost at the same instant.

Dale dashed through the gateway, aiming at the Mustang's windshield. The car ran straight toward him. I heard the rifle's crack and the shatter of glass, and with

238

terror expected the Mustang to careen off at an angle, with Joel slumped over its steering wheel. Instead, at accelerated speed, it kept heading toward the man on foot.

He fired again. Then, too late, he turned and tried to dodge out of the car's path. One end of the car's bumper caught him, tossed him a little way into the air. I had the impression that the upper part of his body came down on that baling wire fence and bounced off it. Then, although I knew he must be lying at the roadside, I could not see him. The mounded graves cut off my view.

The car had stopped. Sick and trembling, still afraid that Joel might have been hit, I put one knee in the gully's sloping side and hoisted myself back into the little graveyard. When I got to my feet I saw that Joel had left the car and now stood at the roadside looking down.

On legs that felt weak I ran past the green camper, out the open gate. Fleetingly I noticed that the Mustang's windshield was an opaque mass of shattered glass, with one bullet hole at a point about two feet above the steering wheel and the other high in the righthand corner. Then I was standing beside Joel.

Eyes closed, face ashen, Dale lay with his head twisted at an odd angle. Until I became aware of slight rise and fall of his chest, I thought he must be dead.

I asked, "Is he going to—"

"I don't know, but I'm pretty sure his neck is broken." He stepped onto the road, picked up the rifle from where it must have flown out of Dale's grasp, and laid it down several yards away from the injured man. Then he looked at the camper. "One of us has to drive back to that horse ranch and phone for police and an ambulance. Can you drive that thing? We can't use the Mustang. All that

239

broken glass is apt to cave in at any moment."

"I'm not sure I can handle the camper. You'd better go and I'll stay here."

Weird as it may sound, considering what Dale was, apparently neither of us felt that he should be left lying alone there like a run-over jack rabbit.

"All right. I'll make it fast."

When Joel had driven off I stood beside the open gate, arms crossed on its top bar and head resting on my arms. I wondered when Dale had come to Las Vegas this second time. Right after he learned we had traced Karen as far as Chicago? Perhaps, but not necessarily. He had not only known where we were headed. He'd also known that, at the rate we were traveling, it would take us four or five days to get there. Nevertheless, he must have flown out to Las Vegas well ahead of our arrival, rented that camper under some false name, parked it beside the road leading to Rancho Mesquite—and waited.

Minutes passed, with no sound except the keening of the wind, and, once, the rustle of some small creature, perhaps a lizard or desert mouse, through a mesquite clump a few feet away from me. Then I heard the camper's engine.

Joel parked the vehicle between the road and the baling wire fence, got out. "I told the police he'd tried to kill us. I also told them I think he has a broken neck, so they're sending a doctor along in the ambulance."

He went to the Mustang, took an old red wool blanket from the trunk, and spread it on the hard-packed earth at the roadside. Seated beside him I said, "I wonder if he would have tried to kill us if we'd turned back toward Las Vegas after we left Rancho Mesquite."

"I don't think so. If we'd done that, probably he would

240

have decided that we had accepted Karen's death as an accident. Oh, he would have followed us for a while to make sure that we didn't stop at the police station in Vegas, but then probably he would have let us go. After all, he knew we could never prove he was responsible for either of those deaths back in Maine. So why run the risk of more murder unless he had to?"

"But instead of going back to Las Vegas we came here to Karen's grave."

Joel nodded. "And that must have made him feel that there was a good chance that we would demand that the grave be opened. And that he couldn't allow."

He paused and then went on, "Carling must have scouted this place sometime within the past few days. He knew that if you had to commit a double murder, this was a pretty good spot for it. He could have stripped us of all identification afterward and tossed us into that gully. Days might have passed before we were even found, let alone identified."

"There would have been the Mustang."

"No problem. These days, they say, the desert is strewn with old wrecks. He could have driven the Mustang far out onto the flats, stripped it of license plates and anything else that might tie it to you and me, and perhaps doused it with gasoline and then set fire to it. By the time either we or the car were identified, Dale could have been almost anywhere in the world."

We sat in silence for several seconds. In the distance, hundreds of feet in the air, some sort of large bird, perhaps a buzzard, circled slowly, black against the late afternoon sky. With an inward shiver I thought of how such a bird, circling above that gully, might have supplied the first indication that Joel and I lay there.

241

I asked, "And Brian and Eunice?"

"What about them?"

"What do you think they are doing?"

"Right now? Probably waiting for their old friend Carling to get in touch with them so they can decide just where in Europe or South America or what not the three of them will get together."

"You mean you think they plan to leave the country? For good?"

"Sure. In fact, there's at least a chance they've already gone. Oh, nobody can prove they helped murder Josephine Andexter, or even that her death was murder. But there's the little matter of having attempted to defraud the Open Land Conservancy of all those millions."

"You think they have enough money to—"

"Spend the rest of their lives abroad? Sure. They have a private income. And in fifteen years of free-loading off Josephine Andexter, they must have been able to save plenty of it."

So maybe they would get away with everything, after all. But at least, I thought, trying to fight down my bitterness, Dale would pay for Josephine Andexter's death, as well as for Karen's and Betty Gadsen's. In fact, he was paying right now.

Again silence settled down. Then Dale made some sort of inarticulate sound half-way between a groan and a whimper. We got up and walked over to him. He hadn't moved, but his eyes were open. They even held a fairly alert expression.

He said, looking at Joel, "How in hell is it you're still alive?" His voice was weak but distinct enough. "I fired twice right through that windshield."

"I ducked real low. If you have to, you can steer just

barely looking over the dashboard."

Sound of sirens on the still air. Dale said, "Police?"

"And an ambulance."

The vehicles stopped in the road. A Las Vegas police car. A Nevada state troopers' car. An ambulance. So silent until moments ago, the place seemed to swarm with uniformed police and with white-coated men from the ambulance. One of the Las Vegas policemen carried the rifle to his car. One of the three white-coated men, apparently a doctor, knelt beside Dale.

Dale asked, "How am I doing?"

The answer was blunt. "Not good. Without touching you I can tell you have a broken neck. If you want to make a statement, it had better be soon."

"Hell, yes, I want to make a statement." For some reason, or perhaps no reason at all, his gaze went to me. "I did most of the planning and most of the work. You think I'm going to end up like this while those two stay alive and out of jail? No way!"

So apparently they hadn't gotten out of the country yet. One of the policemen said, "I'll ride in the ambulance and take his statement."

Two attendants lifted Dale very carefully onto a stretcher. Minutes later the ambulance, with the attendants on the front seat and the doctor and one policeman in back with Carling, made a U-turn on the hard earth at the roadside and started back toward the highway. The state troopers' car followed it.

The remaining policeman said, "You'll have to come to the station house and make a statement too. Better come with me. You sure can't drive that Mustang with its windshield like that. Somebody'll come out and pick up that camper later."

243

"All right. But could we have a few seconds first?"

"I don't see why not."

Joel and I walked past the camper. One of the wooden crosses, I noticed for the first time, had been shattered by a bullet. Hands clasped, we looked down at the grave of Karen Andexter, granddaughter of Josephine Andexter, and once the beloved of twenty-year-old Joel Cartwright. There was no sound but the wind's whisper.

After a minute or two we turned and walked toward the waiting police car.